Chauncey's Blood

A Hiram Robinett Novel of the Civil War

Curt J. Robinette

Second Edition © 2018

Monday Creek Publishing
Ohio USA

ISBN-13: 978-0692045121
ISBN-10: 0692045120

ACKNOWLEDGEMENTS

There are a few people who I want to acknowledge for the support they provided in putting this novel together. Let me start with a short story of how it all began.

In 2015, I received a Skype call from my younger sister Jean Carol and her husband Scott Dittmyer, who live in San Diego. She had decided that now that we were all retired, we needed a project to work on that would keep us all active and engaged. I wasn't that interested with her initial idea, which was to write a book about our grand uncle Hiram Robinett.

The background on our Hiram connection came from my interest in our Robinette Family History. Since 1993, I had pursued, in my little bit of spare time, all the information that I could find on our folks, their brothers and sisters, our grandparents, etc. Not incredibly proficient, I still somehow managed to find out much more information than I ever thought possible. Note that this family information is described in the first two chapters of the book.

As our efforts focused around getting together on

the internet, we debated who we might recruit to help in writing a book. We decided that Jean and Scott would perform research on the time-period and areas of interest that might have impacted southeastern Ohio and more specifically Athens County. Older sister Betty would oversee the project and try and keep us on tract and from killing one another. Scott also accepted the responsibility of being the initial critic, evaluating our writings and making suggestions to keep us enthused yet humble. He kept us quite humble.

As we progressed, it became apparent that the researchers and the primary writer were not in sync as to what the story objective was to be. The researchers, both retired federal investigators, were interested in the facts and were looking for a more historically detailed book focusing on education. As the writer, a former computer geek, I was more interested in telling a story of a young Robinett boy from Ohio who went off to see the world at its ugliest, fight in the Civil War, and make America a better place.

So, long story shortened, the team began to unravel and the book, as I, now on my own, envisioned it, began to take form. We stopped the weekly conference calls and communications about the story. I kept writing, but I tell this story because of the importance of those initial efforts including the extensive research and the impact the events had on the writing of this novel. We got to know our ancestors by writing bios on the primary players and ironing out our different perceptions of who they really were. An example would be family rumor suggesting Hiram's father Ezekiel was a womanizer. In the family lore, the fact that he had been married three times insinuated that there might have been a moral reason for that. Simple but continuing efforts to find the truth, demonstrated that his first two wives died, leaving him with a large family to raise and a convenience to remarry. The child of the third wife assumed his name, making it appear to the casual observer, that he had a child out of wedlock. Not the case. Mystery solved.

Two individuals outside of family played a role in getting this novel written. The first is Linda Cunningham Fluharty, a retired nurse and noted West Virginia Historian. Linda provided my first connections with my grand uncle Hiram and his role in the Civil War and the Battle of Gettysburg. She provided and gave permission to use a formal picture of Hiram in his uniform, and that started my love affair with the man. I have continuously consulted with Linda, ran an initial cut of the story by her and her reaction gave me the confidence to keep going. The second individual, Lorinda LeClain, is the Athens County Library Historian. Her efforts in finding answers and explaining details that this amateur could understand were invaluable. Lorinda, an author herself, also reviewed my story line and gave her approval. I thank Linda Fluharty and Lorinda LeClain for their belief in Hiram Robinett and through him, in me.

I have wondered why writers always acknowledge their family, once they have completed writing a book. Once you have done it, once you put the time and effort involved, it becomes quite clear. To accomplish telling a story properly, figure out how to get it into book form, find a publisher and work to get your product to market, you're quite amazed that you still have a family.

So, I thank my wife, Joy Robinette, for the strength she possesses, the willingness to love me much more than I ever deserved. The willingness to watch me do my thing and my cumbersome attempt to write a book anyone would want to read. She was, as I suspect most mates are, the first to review the book. She told me it had possibilities. Joy is a voracious reader, five or so books a week, so I was surprised and encouraged. A good mother and a great grandmother. An inner beauty that is totally real. We love our three daughters, Christine Marie, Joy Elizabeth and Melinda Francesca. Mindy helped with initial edits.

My sister Betty and Jean Carol for the research, critiques and belief that I could possibly write a novel. My nephew Brian, a retired Navy Chief who never got to see the finished product but was happy if I mentioned his civil war hero, George Armstrong Custer. So, now I have.

There are others I want to thank. My new publisher, Monday Creek Publishing and proprietor Gina McKnight and her staff. They have accepted the challenge of producing the Second Edition of *Chauncey's Blood, A Hiram Robinett Novel of the Civil War*.

CONTENTS

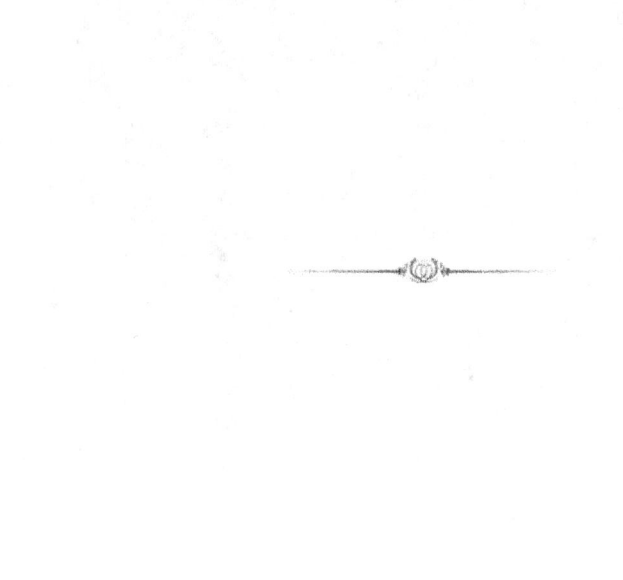

PROLOGUE

In our history, the United States of America has gone to war a dozen times for a multitude of reasons. We fought to gain our independence, we struggled to stay free. The invasion of Mexico was due to the perception of "manifest destiny" by the Polk administration, who wanted Texas and much more. We entered World Wars I and II to save our allies, and we fought to protect our interests. Although debatable, we entered several conflicts when we shouldn't have. Of all the conflicts, battles and declared wars, the most brutal, deadly and divisive for America was the Great Rebellion, the Civil War, which lasted from 1861 to 1865.

This war came at a very critical point in our young history. The country was just beginning to stand on its own. Progress was being made in important areas such as manufacturing, agriculture, tobacco, cotton, transporting and trade of goods around the world, and we were positioning ourselves to become a leader in multiple venues. This national catastrophe threatened to destroy everything thus far achieved, perhaps even the union itself. A war required soldiers and those soldiers came from our cities, towns and villages. Only the rich and powerful were spared, and then, only if they chose to be. The war machine required horses. In 1860, there were estimated to be 2 million horses in the United States. At the end of the war in 1865, there were 180,000 horses remaining alive in all of America.

The Civil War was incredibly brutal, resulting in the loss or ruination of 700,000 American military and civilian lives and impacting every family in our country. This story details the impact of war on two childhood friends from Southeastern Ohio.

Young adventurous boys, both eager to do their part, to seek adventure and discover what the world had to offer. How they handled the situations presented to them would change them forever. Like many others, these young warriors were heroes, one perhaps more conventional than the other.

I hope you enjoy this story of my grandfather's brother and his friend. The novel includes historical and military facts about two very real young men, Hiram Robinett and Robert H. Edwards, from the small village of Chauncey, Ohio.

1: How the Robinette's Arrived in Ohio

Allen Robinet[1], patriarch of the Robinett[2] family line in America, was a 'first purchaser' from William Penn of 250 acres of unlocated land yet to be surveyed in the wilderness of Pennsylvania by the usual deeds of Lease and Release, dated March 21-22, 1681. His property was laid out after his arrival in America under a General Warrant of Survey dated September 9, 1682 from Thomas Holme, Surveyor General, in Providence, later Upper Providence Township, Chester County, now Delaware County, Pennsylvania. The acreage was located just north of the present town of Media (see page 2). His property included an additional city lot in the new city of Philadelphia, which he purportedly never settled.

Allen and his wife Margaret had four children, all born in or around London, England. Allen Jr. (1666) was the oldest followed by Susanna (1668), Samuel (1669) and finally Sarah (1670). It is believed that son Allen and daughter Susanna came to America separately and Samuel and Sarah came with their parents in late 1681 and settled on their newly acquired property.

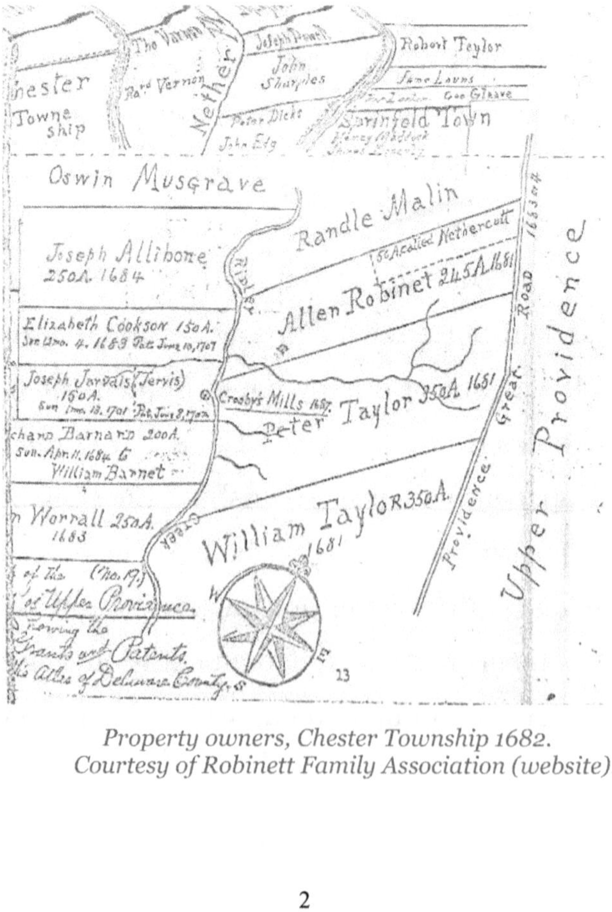

Property owners, Chester Township 1682.
Courtesy of Robinett Family Association (website).

Allen's younger son Samuel married Mary Taylor and they resided on the Allen Robinet property until 1715 at which time they purchased land and moved to East Nottingham Township in Pennsylvania. The next year Samuel also purchased several large plots of land in adjoining Cecil County, Maryland.

Samuel and Mary had nine children, eight of whom lived to adulthood. George was the youngest son of the nine and inherited Samuel's Plantation upon Samuel's death in 1745. George lived there until 1756, at which time he is found in Frederick County, Maryland. Sometime in the late 1760s, early 1770s, he and his brother Nathan moved their families to Murley's Branch, Flintstone District, Allegany County, Maryland. George would spend the rest of his life there, dying before 26 May 1803, the probate date of his will.

George married Catherine (last name unknown) before 1740 and they had eight children who grew to adulthood. The third of four sons, Ezekiel, was born between 1750 and 1755. He and his brothers would eventually and via several different paths move to Athens County, Ohio.

Hiram's great grandfather Ezekiel Robinet, mentioned above, came to Athens County, Ohio from

Murley's Branch, Allegany, Maryland via Brooke County, (West) Virginia. Ezekiel's son, Moses, arrived with his father sometime soon after 1806, settling on what would become known as Robinet Ridge in New Marshfield, Waterloo Township, Athens County. Ezekiel and his wife Mary (last name unknown) had at least 14 children and son Moses and his wife (name unknown) had 13 children. Record-keeping would not become law until 1858 in Ohio. The names of some of these children are not recorded and they likely did not live to adulthood.

Moses named his first born, a son, after his father Ezekiel. This Ezekiel (identified as Ezekiel II) is the father of Hiram, the subject of this story.

2: Structure of the Families

Hiram Robinett was born January 31, 1843, in Waterloo Township, Athens County, Ohio. His father was Ezekiel Robinett, born 1811; his mother was Lucinda Gabriel, born 1808. Both parents were listed in the 1850 Census as having been born in Ohio and both of their families are known to have arrived in Waterloo Township in the very early 1800s. Lucinda's father was Abraham Gabriel and her mother was Mary Polly Higgins.

Ezekiel and Lucinda's children were Andrew Josephus, born 1835; Nancy, born 1839; Hiram; Charlotte, born 1849; and Moses, who was born in October 1851. Lacking supporting evidence of documentation, the gaps between Andrew, Charlotte, Nancy, Hiram and Charlotte suggests the strong possibility other children were conceived of this union but did not survive.

Lucinda died between the time of Moses' birth in October 1851 and September 1857, at which time a single Ezekiel married his second wife, Jane Swift Gibson, herself, apparently, a recent widow.

Jane Swift was born between 1819 and 1822, dependent upon which documents you accept as accurate. Although her parents are known to be John and Jane Swift from Pennsylvania, the specific Swifts are unknown. There is a possibility that Quakers John and Jane Swift of Easton are her parents, with two additional siblings, Richard and John.

Jane married William Gibson in Morgan County, Ohio, on October 20, 1840. In the 1850 U.S. Census, they had two children, James M. born in 1842 and Katherine[3] following in 1848. Two additional boys, Warren G. in 1851 and William H. Gibson in 1853 completed the family. Husband William died and on the 20th of September 1857, Jane Swift Gibson married Ezekiel Robinett II.

The U.S. Census for 1860 showed significant changes. The Robinett and Gibson families had merged. Andrew Josephus married Mary Fitch, and Nancy married Moses Six. Both families were living close by. James M. Gibson was living with a family in Athens. Ezekiel and Jane had their first child, Sarah, born in 1858. They would have two additional children, my grandfather Curtis Godridge in August 1860 and Minnie in 1865.

The same 1860 U.S. Census indicated that Robert H. Edwards was born in 1844 in Dover Township, Athens County, Ohio. His father, William M. Edwards, was born August 8, 1811 in Baltimore, Maryland. His mother, Sophronia N. Finley, was born about 1813 in Pennsylvania. Sophronia's father was born in Pennsylvania. Eliza Ann Findlay, her mother, was born in England in 1790. Sophronia's sister, Nancy, was also born in Pennsylvania in the year 1820.

William and Sophronia Edwards' children included Susan, who was born November 23, 1842; Robert, born October 25, 1844; Mary, who was born in 1846; Frank Morris, who was born in 1849; Charles, born in 1852; and Anna, who was born in 1855.

William was a cabinet maker by trade, noted in the 1850 Census. He and Sophronia maintained a large household, with her widowed mother Ann Finley and Sophronia's younger sister Nancy living with them. Two apprentice cabinet makers plus a carpenter also boarded in the home. In 1853, William was appointed the Postmaster in Chauncey, a position he held until 1856. In 1860, with still a large household, William continued to work as a cabinet maker. Robert was now 16 years old, and was responsible for chores and helping his father.

Between 1860 and the 1870 Census, William owned and operated a dry goods and grocery store in Chauncey.

In the 1880 Census, William, Sophronia and son Charles Edwards lived in the village of Athens. William was landlord of a boarding house; son Charles painted for a living and Sophronia's sister Nancy continued to reside with them. William M. Edwards died September 8, 1885, and his wife Sophronia passed in 1896.

3: Historical Perspective

It is appropriate to give some historical perspective as to what was going on in the United States of America during the period Hiram and Robert were growing up in Southeastern Ohio. One could speculate that most events occurring nationally had little impact on their lives, was unknown or of little significance to them.

James Tyler was the President of the United States when Hiram and Robert were born. Tyler was referred to as *His Accidency* by members of Congress. Being the first Vice President to assume the position of President without being elected was a new experience for everyone. Congress felt that the position was meant to be a temporary solution, but the founding fathers put no provisions in place to elect a new President. Tyler wanted the position and fought strongly to keep it and he was successful. Two significant events occurred during his one term in office. A trade treaty was signed with China that opened the Far East to the western world and Texas became the 28th state, which eventually led to war with Mexico.

Obviously, no one could know that years later, in 1862 during the early stages of the Civil War, former President Tyler would be elected Senator of the Confederate States of America and die in Richmond, a rebel and former Governor of Virginia. The 10th President of the United States became technically a traitor to the United States of America.

During the 1850s in America, the slavery issue was festering and threatening to erupt at any time. Many white Americans were sympathetic to the blacks and were willing to assist those attempting to flee. This was not something new in our country. The War of 1812 is credited for beginning the Underground Railroad (UR) which continued to grow throughout its existence until the end of the Civil War. Whether the British offering freedom and citizenship to fugitive slaves escaping to Canada was a noble cause or meant to disrupt the government of the United States would have been little concern to folks in Southeastern Ohio. Through constitutional mandate, Ohio was a free state and was against slavery and thus sympathetic to fleeing people of color.

Cincinnati was more sensitive to its position as the major port on the Ohio River and the connection for shipping goods both north and south. The economy of the city was critically dependent on the ability to deal with both free and slave states and so was politically handled as appropriately as possible. One could say the almighty dollar ruled over what was just and humane.

The UR offered a pathway to freedom and was supported in and around Athens County, a focal point for runaway slaves trying to flee to Canada. Belpre, Ohio was a major hub on the UR, as was Little Hocking, Washington County. The Horace Curtis House in Little Hocking, later becoming the Sawyer Inn, was the first known UR Station in Ohio, becoming active in 1812. It was located on the Marietta to Chillicothe Pike, which was the first funded highway built in Ohio. The Pike ran to and through Athens and there existed several known UR Stations in and around Athens County.

Athens was a point where fugitives attempting to get to Canada would have turned north towards Zanesville and beyond. It is likely that Hiram's family would have been aware of these events taking place but to surmise that they were influenced by the activities would be speculation to a high degree. However, for someone who has studied Hiram's life and pursuits, I found it certainly conceivable.

Sawyer-Curtis House, Courtesy of Wikipedia.org

4: Growing Up in Athens County, Ohio

Hiram Robinett and his friend Robert H. Edwards grew up in and around the village of Chauncey, in Dover Township, in Athens County, Ohio. In their childhood years, the community was growing rapidly. The salt and then coal mines were flourishing. The opening of the Hocking Canal was making access into and out of Athens County more reliable and affordable as well. The railroad wouldn't be far behind.

More people in the village also meant more things to do and Chauncey was proving to be a good place to live and raise a family.

Hiram, Robert and all the children of this era were expected to carry their load or earn their way. They had daily chores that were significant and necessary for the comfort and existence of the entire family. Basically, every family farmed to the extent required to feed their family. Those who could grow extra, did and often bartered that excess food for other necessities required to live comfortably. Barter was more prevalent than hard money when earning a living.

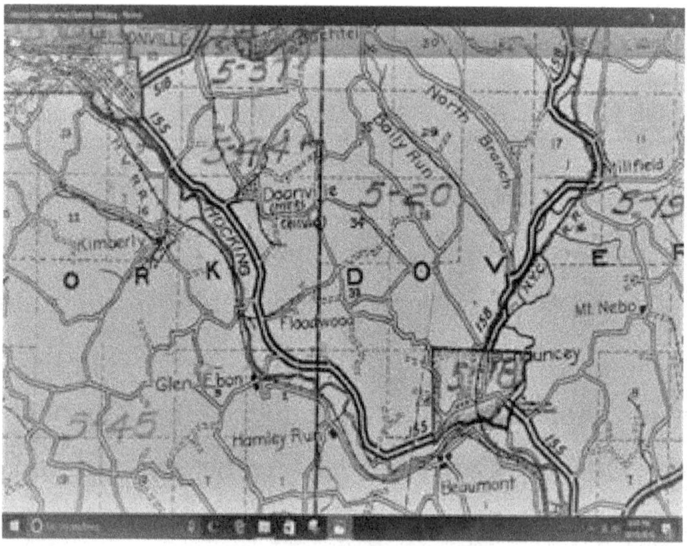

Athens County Census Map

As the children aged, they assumed more responsibilities based on their capabilities and maturity levels. Older girls helped their mothers with the household chores, assisting with the younger children, all of which were in preparation for when they had a family of their own. Keep in mind that most families were large, often six to ten, or even more children. Obviously, the total effort to feed, house and raise a family of this size required effort, planning, cooperation and good fortune. The Robinett and Edwards families appeared to be successful in all these areas.

Cliff Kittle Collection – Facebook.com

Of course, growing up was not all work. There was ample time for play and relaxation and doing the things that kids do. Boys could hunt, fish and of course explore. Hiram and his neighbor Robert had time to get involved in more things than they probably should have but it was mostly harmless fun. They fished, swam in the Hocking River, waded in creeks, rode horses and burros and even tried a calf or two, not with much success.

Other things of interest occurred in Athens County, Ohio, in the 1840s/1850s/1860s and would have created excitement and entertainment for the citizens. Circus and carnival visits to Athens, Chauncey, and Nelsonville were typically exciting times and families would make the trip to town to participate in the fun. Everyone enjoyed the fun, regardless of financial position in life. One 1852 encounter that was reported in the Boston newspaper helped increase the interest in the Circus coming to town.

Festivities could be found in church revivals as well. Believers and those searching for answers would participate in the revival and it would get very exciting and often quite rambunctious. Other citizens and neighbors would attend, either inside the revival tent or outside, wherever they might find a good view of the happenings. Most always, everyone in attendance had a great time and a few of the attendees were saved. Robert always claimed he was saved, from the hill behind the tent. Hiram agreed readily that Robert needed to be saved, however or wherever it might happen.

Life during these years in Athens County was good and the boys had many memorable times growing up.

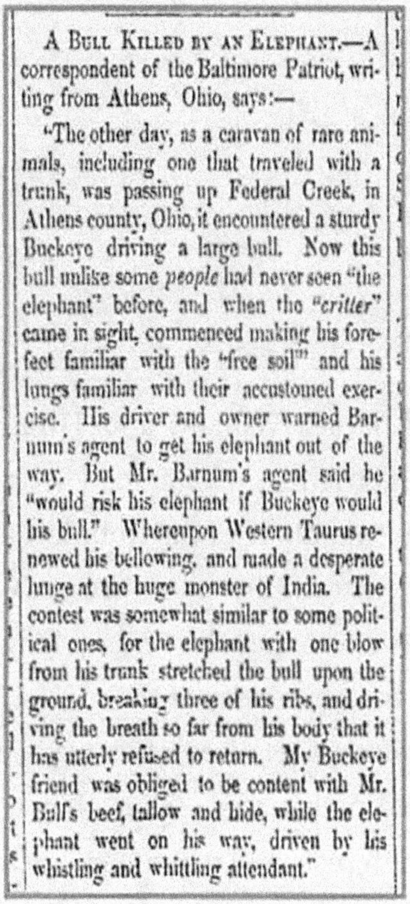

A BULL KILLED BY AN ELEPHANT.—A correspondent of the Baltimore Patriot, writing from Athens, Ohio, says:—

"The other day, as a caravan of rare animals, including one that *traveled* with a trunk, was passing up Federal Creek, in Athens county, Ohio, it encountered a sturdy Buckeye driving a large bull. Now this bull unlike some *people* had never seen "the elephant" before, and when the *"critter"* came in sight, commenced making his fore-feet familiar with the "free soil" and his lungs familiar with their accustomed exercise. His driver and owner warned Barnum's agent to get his elephant out of the way. But Mr. Barnum's agent said he "would risk his elephant if Buckeye would his bull." Whereupon Western Taurus renewed his bellowing, and made a desperate lunge at the huge monster of India. The contest was somewhat similar to some political ones, for the elephant with one blow from his trunk stretched the bull upon the ground, breaking three of his ribs, and driving the breath so far from his body that it has utterly refused to return. My Buckeye friend was obliged to be content with Mr. Bull's beef, tallow and hide, while the elephant went on his way, driven by his whistling and whittling attendant."

Circus in Athens 1852 Elephant kills a bull

5: Mount Nebo – A Mystical Experience

Robert's father William and Hiram's father Ezekiel were good friends. William had been born in Maryland and knew members of the Robinett Family who moved to Southeastern Ohio years before. While he didn't follow them here, they did end up living in the same village for the remainder of their lives. They attended the same church, socialized often and got together to play cards and make music when they could. They shared similar interests and when they heard of The Spiritualists at Mount Nebo[4], they decided to make the short trip over to Millfield and see what it was all about. After some serious begging and pleading, Hiram and Robert were permitted to take the trip with them but would not be able to attend the gathering. That was disappointing but at least a minor win by being allowed to go.

The boys had no idea what to expect. The trip of three miles was made in the evening and the last two miles up to the house was very dark. Others attending were on this road with them and mostly it was the noises of the horse hooves and nervous snorting accompanied by quiet laughter. It was spooky, and the boys loved it.

When they entered the farm, a big bonfire was blazing in the front yard and probably two dozen people were standing around, talking, smoking and waiting for the event to begin. Off to the side of the farm house where the Koon's lived, was a newly constructed structure. It didn't appear that it would hold much more than the number of folks in the front yard, so any hopes that Robert and Hiram harbored about perhaps squeezing in appeared dashed.

Sure enough, that was the case. Suddenly, what sounded like a big bass drum exploded, startling everyone to attention. Jonathan Koons, assumed to be the master of ceremonies, urged everyone who had signed up to attend to enter the building and be quick about it. Once inside, the three windows were shuttered, and the lone door closed tight.

Robert and Hiram settled by the fire on one of several benches and waited, not knowing what to expect. Shortly, the sound of a lone fiddle began to play a solemn melody which was not a familiar tune. After a short minute, other instruments joined in and as each joined, naturally the music became louder. After what seemed maybe two minutes at most the music was so loud that the boys imagined it could easily be heard for several miles. Again, the music had a melody that was not familiar to the boys. It was noisy and it was spooky and Hiram and Robert agreed that everyone who entered the building must be attempting to participate in this effort and with little success.

After maybe fifteen minutes, the noise abruptly stopped. From outside, there was an eerie silence and the boys imagined that it might be over. However, it was at least forty-five minutes before the door opened and the attendees began to exit the building. Gathering again around the fire, Robert and Hiram stood close to their fathers and listened intently. They seemed to be gathering information as well. Others who had been in the room were much more excited and vociferous than the two middle aged farmers. There was talk of flying instruments, human hands that wrote messages from the dead, contact that was made with relatives and friends who had passed over. Neither Hiram or Robert had ever witnessed adults in such an excited stage about such unbelievable events they had apparently just witnessed.

Perhaps as amazing as the reactions of the attendees was the controlled low-key reaction by their fathers. Neither was offering much. It was as if they had agreed not to discuss what they had witnessed until they had time to digest it in perhaps a more settled, less biased environment. The ride back to Chauncey in the dark was quiet with just an occasional comment accompanied by a chuckle or two. The boys were tired but eagerly anticipated hearing exactly what their folks thought of this spiritualistic experience. Obviously, it would have to wait until tomorrow.

At the next morning's breakfast, no one was more excited to hear about the spiritualistic event than Robert. Eagerly seated at the table before anyone else, chores completed, he was eager to hear what went on in the dark room. Once father was seated and grace offered, Robert could wait no longer. "Father, tell us! Tell us what happened!"

William chuckled and waited for Sophronia to

finally sit back down after loading the table with morning vittles. He took a sip of his steaming hot black coffee, just the way he liked it, and he began. "Well, for certain, it was everything we expected it to be and much more. Ezekiel and I were both amazed that farmer Koons could create such an amazing spectacle. It all appeared so real and how ever he was able to make those things happen, it was sure something to see."

Robert, eager with anticipation, almost screamed, "What! What did you see?"

William laughed out loud. "Calm down, I'm getting to it! Did you hear the music, son?"

"Yes, we sure did. You all weren't very good. It was a tune I have never heard before but I don't think it will ever be very popular."

"What if I told you we didn't play those instruments? What if I told you that no one played those instruments? Well, actually no one living played them. Farmer Koons, although he claimed he wasn't Farmer Koons, played the fiddle. The other instruments played themselves. They flew around the room and played themselves. I'm not lying. They were flying. I didn't see any strings, attachments or anything else. They flew around and played all by themselves. Ezekiel agrees. It didn't appear to be a trick. If it was, it was a good one."

Sophronia, who had been quietly eating to this point, commented, "That doesn't sound possible. That's actually quite scary!"

William responds, "You think that was frightening, that was just the beginning. John King, who was our host and talked through a horn, then began talking with attendees and their loved ones who had passed over. He spoke in numerous languages, some of it was understandable and some sounded like gibberish to me. He spoke of things to people that upset them a lot, things that apparently, he couldn't have known but was receiving from the other side. It was unsettling to say the least.

"Suddenly paper and pens were made available on the table and from somewhere, out of nowhere, human hands appeared. They were just hands. No arms, not attached to anything or anyone. These hands moved around the table, allowed guests to touch them, hold them, even shake hands with them. These hands then took up pen and paper and began writing notes to the people. They wrote slowly but when asked to speed up, wrote so rapidly as to fill the entire sheet of paper almost instantaneously, yet the notes were well written and clearly composed. This of course, caused many comments and the room grew quite loud. When John King commanded silence, the hands just as mysteriously disappeared and the spectacle was over.

"I want to tell you that this entire experience was quite a show and that is all that it was. That's what I would like to tell you and probably should, but I can't. I can't debunk anything that happened, not one single event. I can't explain it and I strongly believe that most things in our lives can be explained. So, I must deal with the explanation that apparently not everything in life has an easy answer. Maybe one day, but not just yet."

6: Education - A Key to Success

So, this is how life was in Chauncey, Ohio in the 1850s and early 60s. Robert and his siblings attended school on a regular basis and became good friends with the Robinett and Gibson kids. They attended the same church and had basically the same interests.

In 1860, Hiram was attending his last year of school in Chauncey, Ohio. His mother had insisted that he and his siblings get an education and Ezekiel had continued the tradition in her honor. It was not a problem for Hiram as he loved school and learning. Reading was a passion with him and he borrowed books from the age of ten which was considered by many as an age of responsibility.

His grandfather Moses had given him three Volumes of *Universal Geography or A Description of All the Parts of the World, on a New Plan*, authored by M. Malte-Brun. These books were Hiram's prized possessions and on many occasion, had opened the doors to the world for him. He wasn't exactly certain how many volumes there might eventually be, but he decided that one day he would have them all.

School in Chauncey was continuing to improve and Hiram had seen a great deal in the 12 years he had been attending. This current year Hiram and 23 other children were students in the two-room village school. Mr. Horace W. Deschler was teaching, his first year in the position, and Hiram decided that Mr. Deschler seemed adequately adept as a teacher, well informed if perhaps a little lacking in personality.

A roster of the children from Chauncey, Ohio, (obtained from the 1860 Census) who attended school during 1860 with their ages in parenthesis:

Robinett: Hiram (17), Charlotte (11), Moses (9)
Gibson: Catharine (Katherine) (12), Warren (10), William H (7)

Scoonover: Oliver (10), Daniel (9)

Cestero: Isabella (8), Corloan (7)

Green: John W (9), Asa (6)

Skinner: William (8)

Freeman: Almira (5)

Edwards: Robert H. (16), Mary (13), Frank (11), Charles (8)

Birge: Abigail (14)

Deschler: Charles H. (16), Emily (14), Loveina (11), Olive (8), Clark (6)

At this point in his young life, having finished high school, Hiram anticipated that he would next attend Ohio University in Athens. His thoughts on a career were still in the developmental phase, perhaps he would be a doctor or a lawyer. He was certain he wanted to be more than a farmer.

News of events that were going on across the United States had become more easily obtainable. The Athens Messenger had developed a network for obtaining local news that was sophisticated and reliable. Telegraph lines had filled the news lines at a pace never experienced before. Things were happening in the nation's capital that were described in the local papers, occasionally the very next day. Citizens were more informed and perhaps even a little more involved than ever before. Issues of national importance were being discussed in small villages and towns throughout the country. Candidates for local, state and national elected offices could get their beliefs, ideas and objectives out to the public. Editorials for and against a candidate for president, i.e. Abraham Lincoln, centered around his beliefs concerning slavery and states' rights and set the stage for events that would change America forever.

Hiram, Robert and their families and friends grew up smack dab in the middle of these growing controversies and would suffer the consequences of actions that they had no control of and likely little interest in personally.

That would all change and very soon!

7: War Begins

In 1860, Abraham Lincoln is elected the 16th President of the United States. As threatened, South Carolina secedes and southern states follow. War between the North and South begins.

Rebels firing on Fort Sumter. Courtesy Library of Congress.

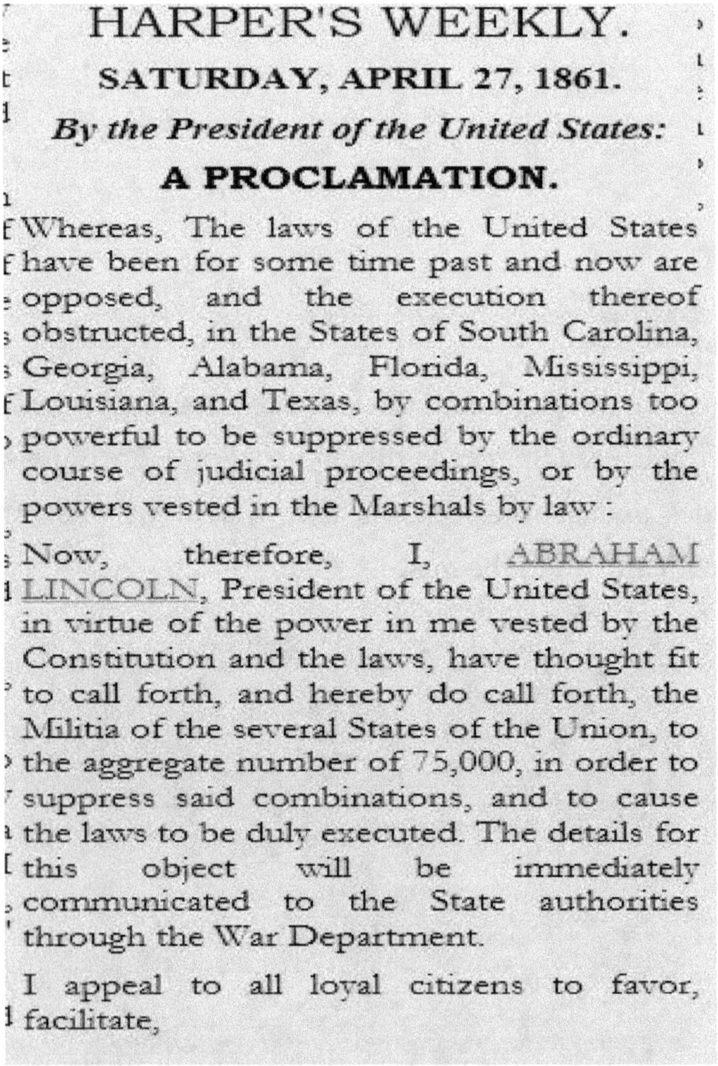

HARPER'S WEEKLY.

SATURDAY, APRIL 27, 1861.

By the President of the United States:

A PROCLAMATION.

Whereas, The laws of the United States have been for some time past and now are opposed, and the execution thereof obstructed, in the States of South Carolina, Georgia, Alabama, Florida, Mississippi, Louisiana, and Texas, by combinations too powerful to be suppressed by the ordinary course of judicial proceedings, or by the powers vested in the Marshals by law :

Now, therefore, I, ABRAHAM LINCOLN, President of the United States, in virtue of the power in me vested by the Constitution and the laws, have thought fit to call forth, and hereby do call forth, the Militia of the several States of the Union, to the aggregate number of 75,000, in order to suppress said combinations, and to cause the laws to be duly executed. The details for this object will be immediately communicated to the State authorities through the War Department.

I appeal to all loyal citizens to favor, facilitate,

Declaration of War - Harper's Weekly

and aid this effort to maintain the honor, the integrity, and the existence of our National Union and the perpetuity of popular government, and to redress wrongs already long enough endured.

I deem it proper to say that the first service assigned to the force hereby called forth will probably be to repossess the forts, places, and property which have been seized from the Union, and, in every event, the utmost care will be observed, consistently with the objects aforesaid, to avoid any devastation, any destruction of, or interference with property, or any disturbance of peaceful citizens in any part of the country; and I hereby command the persons composing the combinations aforesaid to disperse and retire peaceably to their respective abodes within twenty days from this date.

Declaration of War - Harper's Weekly

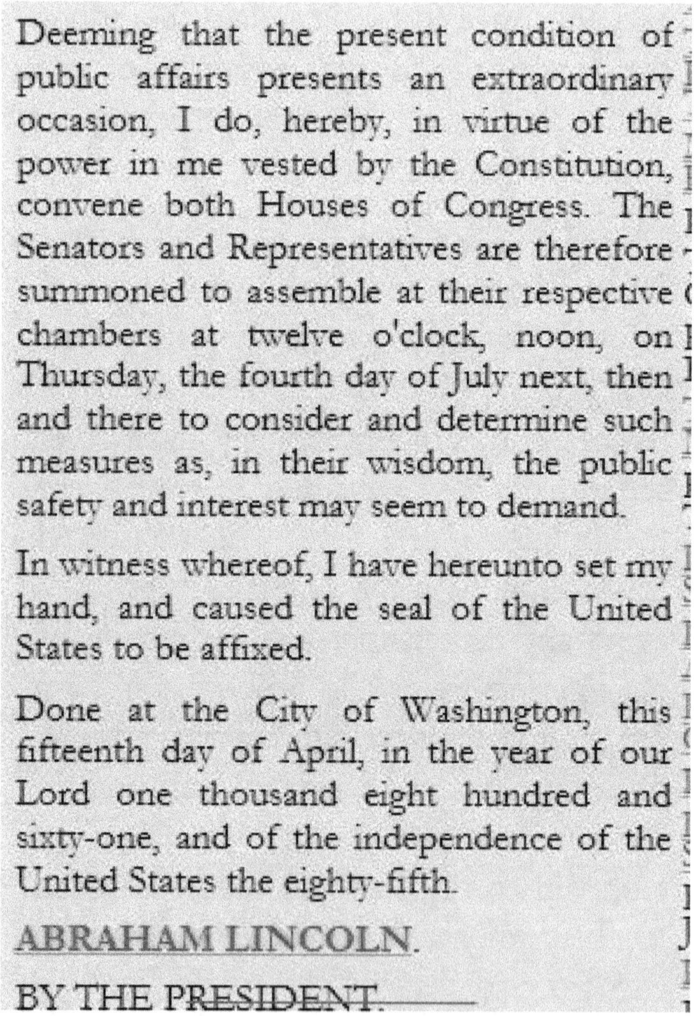
Deeming that the present condition of public affairs presents an extraordinary occasion, I do, hereby, in virtue of the power in me vested by the Constitution, convene both Houses of Congress. The Senators and Representatives are therefore summoned to assemble at their respective chambers at twelve o'clock, noon, on Thursday, the fourth day of July next, then and there to consider and determine such measures as, in their wisdom, the public safety and interest may seem to demand.

In witness whereof, I have hereunto set my hand, and caused the seal of the United States to be affixed.

Done at the City of Washington, this fifteenth day of April, in the year of our Lord one thousand eight hundred and sixty-one, and of the independence of the United States the eighty-fifth.

ABRAHAM LINCOLN.

BY THE PRESIDENT.

Declaration of War - Harper's Weekly

Secretary of War Simon Cameron's communique to the various state governors...

Call to Arms!!!

75,000 Volunteers Wanted

Washington, April 15

The following is the form of call on the respective state Governors for troops, issued to-day:

Sir: Under the act of Congress for calling out the militia to execute the laws of the Union to suppress insurrection, repel invasion, &c., approved February 28, 1795, I have the honor to request your Excellency to cause to be immediately detached from the militia of your state, the quota designated in the table below to serve as infantry or riflemen for three months, or sooner, if discharged.

Your Excellency will please communicate to me the time about which your quota will be expected at its rendezvous, as it will be met as soon as possible by an officer or officers to muster it into the service and pay of the United States; at the same time the oath of fidelity to the United States will be administrated to every officer and man. The mustering officers will be instructed to receive no man under the rank of commissioned officer who is apparently over 45 or under 18 years, or who is not in physical strength and vigor. The quota to each state is as follows: Maine, New Hampshire, Vermont, Rhode Island, Connecticut, Delaware, Arkansas, Michigan, Wisconsin, Iowa, and Minnesota, one regiment each; New York 17 regiments; Pennsylvania, 15 regiments; Ohio, 13; New Jersey, Maryland, Kentucky, Missouri, four regiments each; Illinois and Indiana, six regiments each; Virginia, three regiments. It is ordered that each regiment shall consist of an aggregate of officers and men of 1,780 men.

The total thus to be called out is 73,910 men, the remainder, which constitutes the 75,000 under the President's proclamation will be composed of troops in the District of Columbia.

Source: Encyclopedia ISnare Articles ISnare.com

8: Hiram Steps Up

On April 17, 1861, Hiram Robinette was one of the first men in Athens County to answer the call. He enlisted as a Private in the 3rd Ohio Volunteer Infantry.

Ezekiel walked into the open barn to find Hiram cleaning the cow's stall. The odor of manure deposited during the long winter was not overpowering but needed be removed each spring. Finally, a break in the weather allowed this to be done before the warmer weather arrived which would make the job nearly impossible.

"Take a break, boy. Mother sent you some fresh water from the well. Come on over here and sit. Tell me what it is that's been bothering you of late. We have all noticed that something isn't sitting quite right with you and we might as well get this aired out and resolved."

Hiram removed his heavily caked boots and slowly, almost reluctantly shuffled across the opening between the two stalled sides of the barn. He took a long drink of the water from a tin cup, made a long "Ah, that's good!" and settled on the bench with his father, not too close but close enough.

"So, what's going on between those ears of yours? Someone or something bugging you? Let's get this out in the air, because we have things to do with spring approaching and we are going to be busy. Is it the boys? You know they look up to you, but they can get a bit irritating at times. You did the same thing with Josephus and Nancy and it's only natural."

"No, no! The boys are great! They're young and frisky but they listen to me and usually do what I tell them. Warren does any job well and complete. Billy's younger and I usually must finish up for him but it's not from a lack of effort. They are really good kids."

"You didn't mention Moses. Problems with him? He is the same age as Warren and should be pulling his weight. I see him wandering off with his fishing pole or the shot gun during the middle of the day."

"Moses does his work well, not as well as Warren but still good. He likes to get done and gone and I don't think he is going to grow up to be a farmer. Just doesn't seem like his heart is in it."

"Kind of like you in that respect, I would say. Don't get me wrong but I sense that this is not what you want to do for the rest of your life either."

"That's what I been thinking about a lot recently. Last time in town, I was reading the Rebellion news, along with half the men in Chauncey. They are forming a 90-day Infantry Unit over in Columbus and they are giving $100 sign up bonuses."

"What? You mean joining the Army and going off to this crazy war! I'd sure hate to see you do that. Besides, I would be busy without your help around here. The kids are just that, kids. Who would make sure they did their chores?"

"Lots of fellas are going and all they seem to be doing is training at Camp Jackson, getting ready to fight if necessary. Most think that it will be over before they ever leave Columbus. I turned 18 in January and this would help my transition to an adult. I can think of a lot worse ways for that to happen. Hanging around this part of the country might be one of them."

Ezekiel could tell this was going to be an effort to convince Hiram to stay around. He tried. "There are a lot of good things happening around here in the past couple years. The mines are expanding, the canals and the trains are making it easier to get things in and out of Athens County. Towns are growing as people come in to work and raise a family. Don't you want to have your own place and get a wife and family going?"

"Father? In the same conversation, you're saying I'm still a boy and then want to marry me off to the first woman I find. Or maybe even one you find for me. That's not what I am looking for right now. If I was looking for a girl, I would be looking at Susan Edwards or someone like her. She's good wife material, for certain."

"I seed you were sweet on her. She is a pretty girl and seems to have a good head on her shoulders. Her brother could use some of her maturity, that's for certain."

"Ha! Robert could use a lot of something, for sure! I probably could too, but that's not the point. I'm not looking to marry anyone. I'm wanting to join the Army before the Rebellion ends, so I can get that money every month and see some places to help me decide what I want to do and where I want to do it."

Ezekiel leaned back on the bench, resting against a

stall and re-packed and lit his cob pipe. After a couple puffs of aromatic clouds of white smoke drifted off, he spoke.

"Well, this is not where I expected this conversation to end up. I had no idea that you were thinking of leaving us. Hmm. I don't like having to make quick decisions but with that second puff on the pipe, I realized this is not my decision to make. It's yours. Sounds to me like you have already decided. So, what's next?"

"Pa, before anything else is said, it's important to me that you know how much I love and respect you. You are the best father and a good person. Taking in Jane and her kids was a wonderful thing. She was surely going through a tough time with four kids and no husband. That had to be a real struggle."

"Ha! I appreciate you saying that, but you know, I didn't marry Jane out of the goodness of my heart. She is a striking woman, who seemed to have her eggs in one basket. We needed help as Nancy was too young to handle the pressures she was having to bear. I missed your mama terribly and I know you kids did as well. I was lonely and Jane came into my life at just the right time. So, I didn't do it for just her or them. I did it because it was the right thing to do and I have grown to love her very much. I think you have too."

"I love her for making you happy and taking care of all of us. I have always enjoyed her kids, she has done a good job of raising them and with your help, they are going to do fine. I wish we could get closer to James, but he made his decisions and is living his life. He may regret that lack of family connection someday, who knows?

"Anyhow, I think I have made my decision and believe it is the right one for me. I'm sorry to put you in a bind but I must take opportunities that are available to me if I want to get where I want to be. Besides, there is a possibility that after my 90 days, I might come home and snatch Susan up if she'll have me and buy us a farm somewhere close. We'll have to wait and see how this Army thing plays out."

"So, when does all this happen?"

"I have to be at Camp Jackson in Columbus on April 17, next week this time."

"How are you planning to get there? You walking 70 miles to Columbus?"

"Well, I would if I had to, but there are several men going from town and they said I can catch a ride in their wagon. I know two of them, so I don't expect any problems getting there."

"I reckon that we ought to tell the family. They are all going to be upset to hear you're leaving. Want to tell them now or at supper tonight?"

"I would like for you to tell them at supper, I might have a problem telling this story again. But right now, I need to finish shoveling cow manure for what I hope is the last time ever!"

"Okay, we'll do it at supper. Hiram, let me tell you one thing now, well, maybe a couple. I have always thought that you were special, and you are always going to be. I think you have big things ahead of you and your life is only beginning. You took to education quickly and always have had an inquisitive mind. I even thought you might end up down in Athens at the university. I'm sure you will be a good soldier. You have always been organized and a leader. The kids followed your directions and always want to do well to please you. Those are things, qualities, that will help you throughout your life. I love all my kids, natural born and acquired. I'm proud of them all, their similarities and their differences, all that make them special. Somehow, I have always known that you were going to be the one that makes a difference. Who knows where, who knows how? I know that you will, and I am proud that you are my son. Now, go shovel that cow shit out of my barn! We'll just have to see if it is going to be the last time."

"Yes, Sir!"

Hiram chuckled, sighed and reclaimed his boots and the shovel.

9: Now They All Know

Mother Jane and daughter Kate were busy clearing the table, having finished supper to the disturbing news that Hiram was joining the Union Army. It was shocking to everyone, but Kate was visibly upset.

"Mother, how can Hiram go off and join the army? That is so dangerous. He could really get hurt, even killed."

"I know, Kate, but Hiram is 18 now and can do what he wants. If his father is going to let him go without putting up a fuss, there's not much we can do."

"But Hiram is so important here. He makes sure everything gets done and keeps the boys' minds on their tasks. He does so much himself, he is a hard worker. We'll fall apart without him!"

"The boys will just have to grow a little faster and

assume more responsibility. I am sure that Ezekiel will have the boys toeing the line in no time. He had to do the same thing when Andrew left, and he knows how to handle these things."

"I know, but this time it's different!"

"I noticed that you and Charlotte seem to be taking this more personal than everyone else. I certainly understand Charlotte's concerns. But you! You're really worried about Hiram?"

"I don't want this family to be disrupted. We already lost our father. We have been blessed with a second chance and I don't want this family to fall apart."

"Katie, you don't need to worry about Hiram abandoning us. He is just not that type. Losing your father hurt so badly and we had to survive on our own. Those were happy times and why God lets terrible things like this happen to good people makes me question his compassion. Finding Ezekiel was our salvation and the fact that he feels the same way about us is truly wonderful. He treats you children as equals to his own, don't you think?"

"Yes, Mama, he does. We are all happy here. I don't see why Hiram wants to change all that and go off to war."

"I'm getting feelings here that you really like Hiram, maybe more than everyone else."

"Mother! You say the strangest things. Hiram is family and I don't want to see the family break up. We've done that once and it was terrible. That's all."

"So, that's all there is to it?"

"That's all!"

"Well, okay then. Finish up here and get ready for bed."

"Yes, Ma'am!"

Kate turned away so that her mother didn't see the tears. Jane already had.

10: 3RD OHIO VOLUNTEER INFANTRY

Hiram shared a wagon with three young men and a fella a good bit older. Hiram was always a quiet sort who didn't talk unless he had something significant to either ask or say. The others in the wagon didn't suffer from his affliction. They were excited and talking about anything and everything. Mostly, they talked about why they were going into the military and what they hoped to accomplish. The older gentleman had a college degree and planned on being an officer and obviously, a gentleman. He owned the wagon, so that made him head guy as far as Hiram was concerned. Two of the boys were going to kill Rebs and have a little fun and the 3rd boy was joining to stay out of jail. The Chief of Police in Nelsonville had given him the option, so here he was.

As they approached Lancaster, a train pulled into the station. None of the boys including Hiram had ever seen a train up close so they were excited. The platform in front of the station was filled with people. A large group of young men and some mere boys in uniform were waiting to board and many well-wishers and obviously distraught mothers and family were along to see them off. In general, frivolity was in the air and no one could possibly know how quickly these days of excitement and adventure would turn to sadness and despair. With the intent of joining for a few quick victories and back home to normalcy, reality would soon surface and change the country and the people in it forever.

Hiram soon learned that the uniformed boys were from the Lancaster Guard, a local militia that was formed some ten years before. They drilled and marched in parades and were as prepared as soldiers as one might find in the civilian community. They were volunteering in total and had already been informed that they would be transferring to Washington City to help protect the capitol. Hiram mused that would be a great place to spend his 90 days of service and likely where a lot of the action would be. Hiram boarded his first train ever and spent the remainder of the trip to

Columbus talking with several guard members and was excited when they pulled into the depot.

When they arrived at the Columbus Depot, several Army personnel were waiting. As Hiram, and approximately 100 other young men climbed down from the train, they were ushered as a group to the far end of the platform and told to stand fast. Hiram assumed that meant stay there, so he did.

After about 20 minutes of waiting and watching others move to join the group, a soldier in a crisp dark blue uniform addressed the men.

"I am Captain Fox of the 3rd Ohio Volunteer Infantry and the United States Army. I am here to assemble you volunteers and deliver you to Camp Jackson. At Camp Jackson, you will begin your transition to the 90-day forces of the U.S. Army. I am sure you are here for a varied number of reasons, be it patriotism, adventure, or simply to get away from home. Let me assure you that while you may experience all those emotions during your tour of duty, there is but one reason you are here. We, jointly, are here at the request of the President of the United States, Abraham Lincoln, to end this rebellion and restore the United States to its former glory. We will do that. We will do that quickly and hopefully without a tremendous loss of life.

"The first military event that you are going to experience is falling in and marching over to Camp Jackson, which is approximately two miles from here. We will assemble the Lancaster Guard as the first squad and the rest of you will form up behind them in the similar formation and we will get started. This is your first opportunity to make a good impression with the General Officers at camp, so stay in line, keep up and try and appear like you know what you're doing. If we get there in time, they should be serving supper. If we don't, it may be awhile before you eat again. Form up!"

The Lancaster Guard looked sharp and were quite impressive. The remainder of the group was anything but. They did manage to arrive at Camp Jackson about the same time as the first squad and it wasn't nearly as far as two miles sounded at the Depot. They had a few reprimands from what they would later learn was a Sergeant for talking while marching, but after he demanded their attention, they got the message.

Camp Jackson looked good, rows of white canvas tents, several large new buildings which turned out to be mess halls and administration buildings and the Commanding Officers of the OVI temporary headquarters. Hiram found out later that this land had been a designated park for the City of Columbus, donated by Doctor Lincoln Goodale, who owned a great deal of property in the north end of the city. He remembered that he had been here once as a child, but he was not aware that Dr. Goodale had dictated that this land could not be used for any other purpose or ownership would revert to him. When Governor Dennison had Goodale Park converted to be used as Camp Jackson, it was with the knowledge that it was temporary until a more permanent camp (Camp Chase) could be prepared. By June, Camp Chase had opened, and all military operations were transferred there. Camp Jackson once again became Goodale Park.

In the meanwhile, it was approximately four in the afternoon, and the weather was beginning to chill significantly. There were a multitude of events that needed to occur this first day in camp, if possible, but the Captain humanely directed the volunteers to the Mess Hall and gave them 40 minutes to eat and reassemble.

The long tables were set with a large variety of foods and flaming hot cooking ranges were preparing more. The food was varied and good and Hiram found himself thinking, this might not be so bad. He would find himself reflecting on this initial impression many times over the next four years, but for now, he dug in. He knew he ate too much, but he wasn't certain how often the Army fed folks.

Reassembling, the Captain called them to order. "Men, he began, tomorrow morning the Commanding Officer of Camp Jackson will be here to welcome you and to administer your enlistment into the United States Army. At the completion of that act, you will officially be committed to serving your country for at least the next three months. Dependent upon the actions of the enemy and the duration of the Rebellion, you may be given the opportunity to continue serving. At this point in time, the Secretary of War expects that the insurrection will be under control if not over. Order will be restored and you all will be released to go home and resume your lives.

"Tomorrow and the next few weeks will be extremely busy. There is much to be done to prepare you to be a soldier in our army. Reveille will be at 04:30 and for those of you who don't know what reveille is, you will no doubt learn tomorrow at 04:30. The mess hall will be open at 04:45 and you are expected to get there, get fed, and ready to assemble back here at 05:15. Stragglers will not be tolerated. Dependent upon when the CO gets here for his official orientation, we will be issuing uniforms and at least attempt to make you look like soldiers.

"For the remainder of this evening, Sergeant Wilcox and Corporal Hanning will assign you to your home away from home and issue temporary bedding for tonight. You are urged to take this opportunity to write home and inform your family and loved ones of your safe arrival at Camp Jackson. Writing materials for this purpose will be made available on this one-time basis. From this point forward, you will be expected to provide your own.

"Once again, I welcome you to Camp Jackson and commend you on volunteering to support your country in this time of need. Get a good night rest and reassemble here in the morning. Sergeant Wilcox, take command!"

The gruff deep voice of the Sergeant was easily heard by the 120 men assembled in the clearing.

"At this point, beginning with the first man of the Lancaster Guard, I want you to count off by eight's. When we get to the berthing tents, the first eight will be assigned to the first tent, and we will continue in this manner until everyone has a place to sleep. Corporal Hanning will be your point of contact if you need writing materials and additionally you will give him your letters to be mailed tomorrow. Do not miss this chance to write, because as you will learn in the next 90 days, you will not always be in the position to stay in touch with your loved ones. I urge you to take this opportunity. For those of you who cannot write, find someone to do it for you. For the ones who can, help your fellow soldier because working together could one day save your life.

"One piece of advice and this is the last chance for you to consider it. You will be sworn in tomorrow morning and be a member of my army. If you do not like what you have seen or decided that you made a mistake, this evening would be a good time to depart. No one at the gate will stop you but you must find your own way home. However, if you leave the camp for any reason tonight and attempt to return, you will not be given entry. So, unless you intend to depart for good, do not leave the confines of this camp.

"One more thing, there will be no lights in the tents after 22:00. The camp fires need to be maintained but no candles or lamps lighted after that time. 04:30 comes early and you have a busy day tomorrow so get as much rest as you can. Okay. Attention! Count off!"

The next morning did come early and was accompanied by a blaring bugle and a bellowing Sergeant. It had snowed a light dusting and was beginning to rain. We were encouraged in very nice tones to get up, get dressed, get to breakfast and assemble immediately after to begin our adventure.

Breakfast was every bit as good as supper, and Hiram was satisfied with his choices so far. He thought, *if the rest of the Army is like eating and sleeping, this could be okay.*

Upon reassembling, the troops (Hiram assumed they were now troops) were informed that the Camp Commanding Officer would be addressing them shortly and administering their oath of enlistment. The Sergeant dropped the hint of a possible visit by Governor Dennison, however, that failed to materialize.

Colonel Moore gave a rousing speech concerning President Lincoln's need for support from the State of Ohio and how we would be prepared to give him our very best, our bravest and most capable young men to put an end to this rebellion by the misguided southern states. He reminded all that this is not a battle for northern supremacy, nor for slavery, but to demonstrate that the United States must be maintained at all costs. He assured them that this 90-day effort would likely be what is needed but that should it require longer time and effort, the good people of the State of Ohio would be there to answer the call.

After a good ten minutes of rousing cheers and general patriotic enthusiasm, the group was called to order and administered the enlistment oath, repeating their names and committing to serving their country in this time of need.

About ten o'clock they were given a 15-minute smoke break before reassembling, being divided into groups of 100 which formed a company in the 3rd OVI Regiment. Hiram became a part of Company C and training began. For the next six days, the routine became reveille, exercise, breakfast, drill, drill, lunch, drill, drill, supper, necessary camp site maintenance, guard duty, letter writing, lights out, go to sleep. Wake up, do it all again and again. On that first day, between all the drills, uniforms were issued, shoes that sort of fit were selected, and equipment was issued. No guns or ammunition were available at the time.

On the morning of the seventh day of training, the troops, including Hiram, received orders that they would be transferring to new Camp Dennison, just outside of Cincinnati. They were to be a part of the 1500-man initial work force to help Captain Rosecrans establish the camp and prepare for training, billeting and relocation of thousands of volunteers in Ohio's effort to support the war.

Rosecrans laid out the camp via survey around April 24, 1861. The first post commander was M. S. Wade, a Cincinnatian who was a former general in the Ohio Militia.

Boarding the Little Miami Railroad train mid-afternoon on April 25th, the soldiers enjoyed a three-hour trip to Germany, a small town 17 miles north of Cincinnati. Camp Dennison was to be built on both sides of the railroad tracks, so when the train stopped, they were at the middle of their destination.

Camp Dennison ohiocivilwar.org

The next 90 days turned into 119 days for Hiram. As a hard worker, with adequate education and much common sense, Hiram was recognized as an asset in getting assignments done quickly, appropriately and without the need of direct supervision. From strategically locating and building latrines, assisting in the building of multiple structures including the temporary Camp Dennison Hospital, Hiram proved an asset. One set of skills honed here, the planning and handling of logistics needed in such a major effort, would serve Hiram well once he took to the field. He demonstrated the ability to organize, direct people and supplies to where and when needed, both essential qualities in a fast-moving war effort. Hiram was quick to realize and appreciate the many things that his father had taught him growing up on the farm, as they readily applied to his new tasks.

Hiram passed on enlisting in the three years or duration of the war opportunities, stayed where he was, doing what he enjoyed and learning skills that he hoped would aid him in the future. He was honorably discharged on August 14, 1861, and returned home to Chauncey and the farm.

11: Company E, First West Virginia Cavalry[5]

Last April, when Hiram committed to the 90-day 3rd Ohio Infantry, Robert wanted to do the same. His father forbade it until he turned 18 and Robert was counting the days. Upon Hiram's return to Chauncey, they had lengthy discussions concerning what they should do next. Hiram spent the remainder of the summer of 1861 helping his family on the farm and watching the news with interest and concern for the lack of progress being made. When notification was posted in Chauncey that Captain Harris would be forming a company of cavalry soldiers in Parkersburg in January 1862, Hiram decided this was the opportunity that he had been waiting for. His observations at Camp Dennison had convinced him that the foot soldier was at a distinct disadvantage, both in combat and in the simple but extremely arduous task of getting to the battle. Simply, the Cavalryman seemed much more versatile in battle and indeed more likely to survive the war. While not verbalizing this fact, Hiram realized that if retreat became necessary, hanging on to a galloping horse seemed far more expeditious than running in ill-fitted government issued boots.

Robert's father agreed that this would be preferable to being in the trenches and more importantly in the line of fire.

The young men agreed that they would travel down to Parkersburg and see about enlisting in the newly formed (West) Virginia Cavalry after the first of the year. Early January, there was a break in the weather. January 7, 1862, finds Hiram in Parkersburg, Virginia. Robert struggled but finally his father relented, and Robert joined Hiram on the 24th of January.

The journey that they were beginning would change their young lives forever. They would be forced to become men before their times, see things they never imagined in their worst nightmares, and make decisions that they would be held accountable for the rest of their lives. They joined the war to save the Union. It would cost them dearly.

Joining /Membership

Courtesy of Frontiernet.net

Company E with Captain Harris in command had been formed in September 1861 in Parkersburg. The end of October, they were sent to Clarksburg, West Virginia, to join the regiment, commanded by Colonel Anisansel. The main duties for about three months were drilling and horse guard, and camp guard. It was near the end of this training when Hiram and Robert made it to Clarksburg. Hiram, having prior service with the Ohio Infantry was considered far enough along to learn cavalry strategy, so he moved right into the company. Robert, lacking any experience, was assigned as a teamster for the regiment.

Robert was happy with this assignment. It kept him busy, contributed to the war effort, with minimal dangers, and the primary importance to him, he wasn't asked to kill or harm anyone. He didn't consider himself a pacifist at all, but it just didn't make sense to Robert to ask so many young men to die for something that didn't involve them; most of them didn't understand or even care about. Robert wanted to keep the Union intact but there had to be a more reasonable way to accomplish saving old glory. He would do his part, even die if need be, but that didn't mean that he agreed with it and he certainly didn't like it.

Hiram, on the other hand, was cut from a different piece of cloth than Robert. Hiram enlisted as a Private, but he had no intention of staying in that position. He assumed correctly that his previous three months' service would help acclimate him to the military lifestyle but training with the 1st Cavalry was of course significantly different. The regiment was engaged in scouting, picket and outpost duty and guarding the Baltimore & Ohio Railroad in West Virginia until March 1862.

Hiram liked the military way of life. The strategy involved, the tactics, the hardships and challenges were all part of the attraction to him. Not a war monger by any means, but he understood the costs associated with protecting your interests and he firmly believed that he was fighting for the good of the Union and to free people living in forced servitude. Once this war was won, Hiram was already thinking that this might be a career for him. He felt certain that he could advance and eventually be a leader and truly make a difference. After the war, he would pursue nomination to the Military Academy. He admittedly had big dreams. Hiram wanted to accomplish something.

Robert was a regimental teamster for the better part of three months. When he joined Company E, he admittedly was behind in training and skills. On March 1, 1862, as Robert got a horse, Hiram was appointed

Quartermaster Sergeant, replacing Robert L Warren who was ill in the hospital in Beckley. Hiram was dual hatted, serving additionally as Commissary Sergeant. He referred to himself as Commissary Sergeant, however the Regimental records referred to him as the Quartermaster Sergeant for Company E. When Warren returned two months later, he was assigned to the Ambulance Team, indicating that Hiram was doing well in the position. As company Quartermaster Sergeant, he was under the direction of the company Commander and the First Sergeant. He was responsible for the company wagon and all the property it contained, including the tents, the company mess gear, the company desk, the company library, the ordnance, the subsistence provisions, and the company tools (blacksmith, carpenter, gunsmith, etc.). He was further charged with overseeing the camp set-up of the tents and picket lines. He inspected the company horses and mules, and reported any problems to the Veterinary Surgeon of the Regiment. He was also responsible for acquiring the fuel (wood), forage for the horses, and straw for bedding. These would normally be drawn from the supplies of the Regimental Quartermaster, along with replacements for uniforms and equipment. When not available, the company Quartermaster Sergeant was responsible for forage parties to acquire them. The company Quartermaster Sergeant was required to sign for the uniforms and equipment that were in his custody. Similarly, before disbursing these items to a soldier, he required a signature of receipt, countersigned by an officer. The rank of company Quartermaster Sergeant was not a command position, although he was required to know the drills, and the duties and responsibilities of the line NCO's. He was a member of the company, and his name was recorded next after the First Sergeant on the company rolls. During combat, his place was safeguarding the company wagon and its supplies. He was generally required to fight only in defense of the company property. In an extreme emergency, he could be used to replace a fallen line NCO, but this was extremely rare. His was one of the more important and hectic jobs in Company E, but Hiram was up to it.

The picture that follows is the in-the-field setup. QMSGT Robinett held this position from March through December 1862.

Source: www.archives.gov

Robert, in the meantime, was settling into being a horse soldier. It wasn't bad. Riding his horse as opposed to all the soldiers he passed marching for miles on end made it simple to determine they had made the correct choice.

The skirmishes and running battles happened quickly and typically if things got too hot, they could and would high tail it out of there. In a serious fight, the horses were the first things to go and Robert couldn't imagine how many would die during this war.

The numbers were staggering (1.8 million killed). At the end of the Civil War, there were an estimated 40,000 horses remaining in the entire USA.

Company E was very active after March 1, 1862. They participated in multiple actions, battles, engagements, and skirmishes. Hiram and Robert participated in the following actions and more:

May 1862: Participated in the Battle at McDowell, west of Staunton, Virginia. Under Fremont's Command, battle was lost to Stonewall Jackson.

June 8, 1862: Participated in the Battle of Cross Keys. Under Fremont's Command, battle was lost to Stonewall Jackson.

In the middle of all this action, Hiram received a letter from his father letting him know that his uncle Curt had enlisted as a blacksmith with the 75th Ohio Volunteer Infantry. His uncle John had already enlisted in September of 1861, so Chauncey was well represented by the Robinett family.

August 9, 1862: Participated in Battle of Cedar Mountain (Slaughter Mountain). Under Major General Sigel's Command, battle was lost to Stonewall Jackson.

August 22 - 25, 1862: Participated in the First Battle of Rappahannock Station. Under General Pope, lost battle to Stonewall Jackson.

August 28 – 30, 1862: Second Battle of Bull Run (Manassas). Under General Pope, lost battle to Robert E. Lee.

In late December 1862, Lt. Col. John Knopps recommended, among others, that S. W. Knowles[6] be advanced to 1st Lieutenant and Adjutant of Company E and that Hiram Robinett take his position as 2nd Lieutenant. Those recommendations were approved and took place in January 1863. On January 18, Hiram was promoted to 2nd Lieutenant. This position became available with the promotion of Sidney Knowles to 1st Lieutenant. Sidney was also from the Chauncey area (Hock Hocking) and it is possible that they knew each other before joining the Army.

As most young men would do, Hiram quickly found a photographer and posed for the camera as a new 2nd Lieutenant in Company E, First Regiment, Virginia Volunteer Cavalry. He was obviously one proud fellow. Pictures were sent home and made the rounds in Chauncey, Ohio.

One of the first official acts Hiram performed as 2nd Lieutenant was to join in recommending the appointment of George W. Burgess as sutler for 1st West

Provided by Linda Fluharty@lindapages.com

Virginia Cavalry Regiment. Burgess was approved. He followed the Regiment and provided items that they might need or want in the field or in the garrison and sold food, drink, and supplies. The Articles of War prescribed that persons permitted to sutler must supply the soldiers with good and wholesome provisions or other articles at a reasonable price, i.e. such as writing supplies. Once approved, the sutler had a captive audience in the field. Good quality spirits were also available. However, he was prohibited from selling alcohol to the enlisted men.

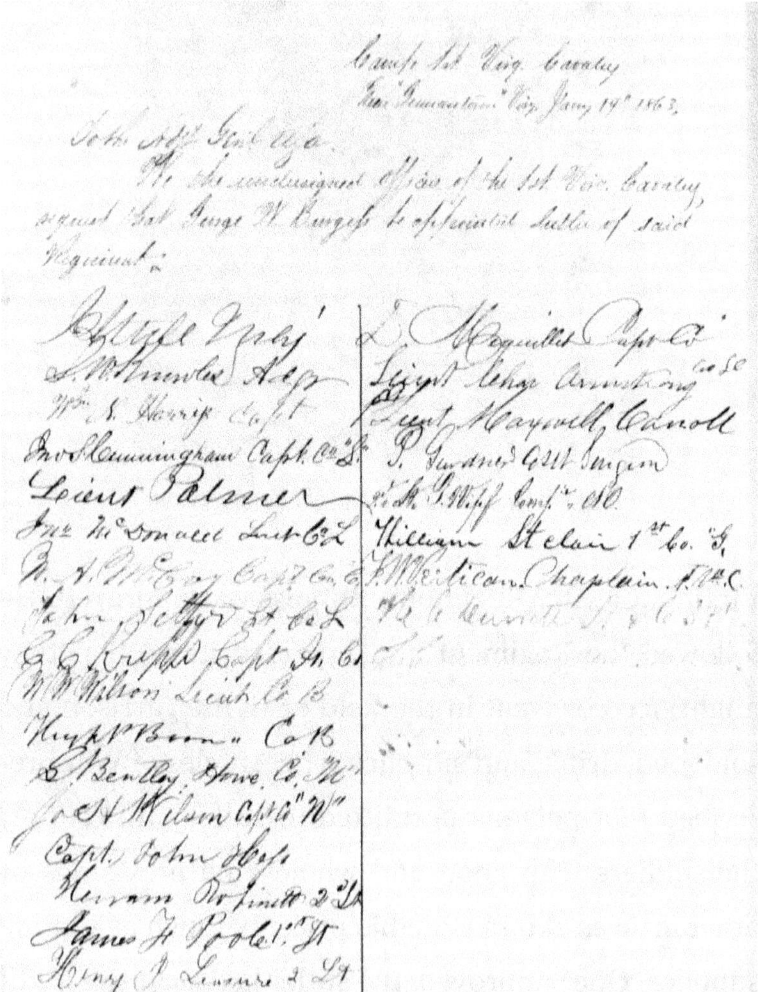

Camp 1st Virg. Cavalry
Near Germantown Virg. Jany 14th 1863.

To the Adjt Genl. U.S.A.

We the undersigned Officers of the 1st Virg. Cavalry request that George W. Burgess be appointed Sutler of said Regiment:

[illegible] Maj
S. W. Knowles Adj
Wm. S. Harris Capt
Jno. S. Cunningham Capt. Co. "L"
Lieut Palmer
Jno. McDonald Lieut Co. L
[illegible] Capt. Co. E
John [illegible] Lt Co L
C. C. [illegible] Capt A. Co
W. W. Wilson Lieut Co B
Hugh P. Boon " Co K
[illegible] Bentley [illegible] Co. "M"
Jos H. Wilson Capt Co "M"
Capt. John [illegible]
Hiram Robinett 2d Lt
James H. Poole 1st Lt
Henry J. [illegible] 2 Lt
[illegible]
[illegible] Second Lieut

[illegible] Capt Co [illegible]
Lieut Chas Armstrong Co [illegible]
2d Lieut Maxwell Carroll
S. Gardner Asst Surgeon
[illegible]
William St Clair 1st Co. "G"
[illegible] Chaplain 1st V. C.
[illegible]

Source: www.archives.gov

Civil War Sutlers Tent

Source: www.archives.gov

Source: www.archives.gov

For a great number of soldiers, the Army was their first extended stay away from home and family. Many of the soldiers wrote letters every chance they had and looked forward to hearing from loved ones. Hiram enjoyed receiving letters and informing family of his adventures.

Hiram wrote home in response to sister Charlotte's letter....

January 1863
Camp 1st Virginia Cavalry, near Germantown, VA
Shallottie,

I received your letter yesterday and was very happy that you responded so quickly. Sorry to hear about your old dog, but he sure had a long life so don't be too sad. He had plenty of fun chasing critters, so he can rest now and let the others have a turn.

Glad that this finds most of you doing well. Things are o.k. here in camp but it is cold and damp. Germantown is not so different from Chauncey, temperature and weather is similar. I had hoped it would be a bit warmer, but I am dressed warm and I am dry. Dry is the most important thing because once you are wet, you cannot get comfortable whatever you do.

We were thinking that this was going to be our winter billet but are now hearing rumors that we might be moving up to support the Capital. I like Washington City as we live better when we are there. Of course, with my promotion, I won't oversee feeding the boys anymore, so I hope my replacement does a good job. There is always a lot going on in the city and the word on how the war is progressing is always available. Many times, out in the field, you don't hear anything and wonder if you are all alone. But then the Rebs show up and you know that you're not.

I need to end this soon, as I still have some duties before sleep. Tell Mose that I'll write him next. Tell sweet Kate, Warren and Billie to stay safe and you do so as well. Give Father and Mother Jane a hug for me. Be sure and let me know if you hear from Uncle Curt. If he is anywhere close, I would love to see him. Same for cousin Stineman.

Till next time, I remain,

Your loving brother,

Hiram

12: A Fateful Trip North

From January to April 1863, the 1st West Virginia Cavalry was kept busy providing for the Defense of Washington, D.C. Hiram especially enjoyed this duty and found himself attracted to the excitement and hubbub associated with big city life. He found that as an officer, he had a few privileges unavailable when he was a mere enlisted man. He remained close to several of the enlisted men, especially his childhood friend Robert. Hiram wasn't certain that Robert was cut out for military life but believed in giving him every chance and any assistance he could to be successful. He knew that Robert marched to the tune of a different drumbeat but sometimes Hiram wondered if maybe Robert had lost at least one of his drum sticks.

In May and June 1863, the 1st West Virginia Cavalry

was assigned to Stahel's Cavalry Division, 22nd Army Corps. Hiram and the Regimental officers met General Stahel and Hiram heard the General was looking for a clerk.

Seemingly out of the blue, Robert was ordered to report to Brigade Headquarters to be assigned as Brigadier General Stahel's clerk. How authorities knew that Private Edwards possessed the skills necessary to support the general remained a mystery. Robert wondered if perhaps Hiram thought this would be a safe place for him.

He saw immediately that there were benefits to hanging around a General, but he would have liked to have remained in the field. This clerking business also was hard work. Maintaining administrative files and records, recording formal musters, making untold numbers of copies of correspondence, orders, Robert used an unending supply of paper, ink and quills. He served in this position until mid-June 1863.

In June, they were assigned to General Pleasanton's 1st Brigade, 3rd Division, Cavalry Corps, Army of the Potomac. Rumors had reported General Lee was moving north for a major push to turn the tides of war. The 1st Brigade began moving north as well. As always, their concern was to stay between the Rebels and Washington.

Major General J.E.B. Stuart's Confederate cavalry which was riding north to get around the Union Army of the Potomac, attacked the 1st Virginia Volunteer Cavalry regiment, driving it through the streets of Hanover, Pennsylvania. Brigadier General Elon Farnworth's brigade arrived and counterattacked, routing the Confederate cavalry, nearly capturing Stuart himself. The Confederate General soon counterattacked. Reinforced by Brig. Gen. George Armstrong Custer's Michigan Brigade, Farnsworth held his ground, and a stalemate ensued. Stuart was forced to continue north and east to get around the Union cavalry, further delaying his attempt to rejoin General Robert E. Lee's army, which was then concentrating at Cashtown Gap, west of Gettysburg.

The 1st day of July was uneventful for Company E. Likewise, on the 2nd, a few minor encounters with Reb Cavalry who were likely doing the same, trying to figure out what to do next. Late in the day, the Regiment received orders to join up with General Kilpatrick who was located just south of Devil's Den where they will confront the enemy's entire right wing on the 3rd of

July.

13: ROBERT'S ADVENTURES BEGIN

Early the morning of July 2nd , Robert was sent out to scout with Corporal Dropsy. Less than two miles from their base camp, they encountered a mounted group of six confederate cavalrymen, apparently doing the same. Hidden from view, the Corporal had the idea to deposit a Ketchum grenade amongst the Rebs. As with many of his efforts, this plan went awry as he dropped the grenade. Before they could retreat, the bomb goes off and Dropsy was distributed amongst the white oaks and the evergreens. The Rebs skedaddle as Robert was blown from his saddle.

He awoke to find that it was dark. Dazed and not certain where he was, he found the remains of Corporal Dropsy and two dead horses and saw that he could not even salvage his saddle and gear. "What a hell of a mess" came to mind and he had no idea of what he should do next. Deep in the woods and not knowing whether the Union or the Rebs controlled the area, he sought shelter and seclusion until daylight could help him get his bearings.

Robert awoke to the sounds of a wagon and horses. Cowering in his cover, he could see what appeared to be a family departing the area. Still feeling the trauma and having a wave of cloudy desperation sweep over him, he waits until they were well past him. Running or stumbling as fast as he could in his condition, he jumped on the back of the wagon and secured himself under the canvas cover. His thought: "A ride to somewhere would be better than a walk to nowhere." Almost immediately, he fell asleep.

While Robert was sleeping in the wagon, his brigade, following orders, moved north west towards Gettysburg. Any patrols deployed were expected to catch up when they could.

Later, Robert was awakened by the sound of a young boy's voice yelling for his father. The wagon stopped and Robert tumbled out from under the tarp. He was surprised to discover that he can barely put weight on his right leg and shocked to see that his boot was covered in dried blood. Apparently, the grenade had paid more attention to him than he had realized.

A middle-aged man dressed in coveralls stood over him, a shotgun held casually yet warily in his right hand. "Who are you, soldier and what are you doing in my wagon?"

"Don't shoot, sir! My name is Robert Edwards and I am with the First West Virginia Cavalry. I got hurt in the woods and I didn't know what to do. I do know that I am tired of this fighting and don't think that I can do this anymore."

"Well, for sure you can't fight for a while with that foot of yours. You can ride with us to Taneytown, but you're going to have to turn yourself in. I can't be harboring a deserter, that's for certain. The name is Wilburn Booth and we are headed to Towson to stay with relatives until this fighting is over. I can't continue trying to farm when everything I produce is taken by soldiers from one side or the other. I am trying to feed my family and losing everything to support this fight will not feed us. I am getting out until the war ends and hopefully we will have something to come back to."

Robert replied, "I'm happy for the help and the ride! I'll get out in Taneytown and see if I can find out where my regiment is. If it's okay, I'll try and get a bit more rest."

"Well, cover up. I don't want no trouble!" Mr. Booth climbed back onto the wagon. "Gid up horse!"

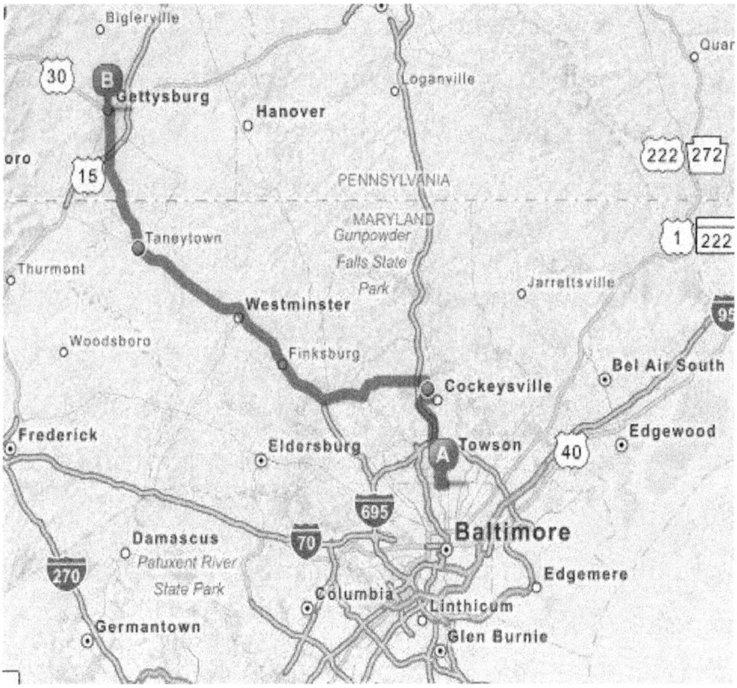

Courtesy Google Maps

When the fever broke, Robert awoke to the most beautiful eyes he had ever gazed into. He had not known that he was sick, but he knew that he was now well. For three days, he was totally out of his senses. He felt nothing and he remembered less. He did not know where he was, or where he had been. He knew only one thing for certain. This was the most beautiful person he had ever seen up close. She appeared busy and unaware that he was awake, so he could stare without embarrassment, which he did. Blond curls surrounded her face and rested on her chest. Perhaps he had died and this was heaven. Then he decided this wasn't heaven because she certainly would not be available to him. God would have reserved this angel for himself.

When Robert accidentally groaned, those beautiful blue eyes jumped directly and locked on his.

"Well, you're awake! Good! How do you feel? We thought we were going to lose you several times. Are you in pain?"

Robert responds. "Who are you? Where am I? I've been sick? What's your name?"

"Whoa! Slow down! One question at a time. My name is Melinda Booth, but I go by Mindy. We are in Towson town, Maryland. You came in the back of our wagon, unconscious and half out of your mind. We brought you all the way from Gettysburg with us. Father wanted to leave you in Taneytown, but I wasn't having it. I knew that I could take far better care of you than the over-crowded hospital there. There were hundreds, if not more, wounded soldiers there from the slaughter at Gettysburg. I was concerned that they would just let you die, so I cared for you and here you are."

"I was sick? What was wrong with me?"

"You had a severe wound with a big chunk of metal just below your right knee. You're lucky you didn't lose your leg. We found a veterinarian to fix your wound in Westminster. He had just helped a cow in distress. Father wanted to leave you there as well, but I convinced him that was not happening!"

"Ha! So, you're not only pretty but you're a savior as well. Thank you! So, what is this place we're in?"

"It's Ady's Hotel. It is owned by a friend of my father's cousin, Edwin Booth. We are staying here until we find a home. Father has arranged for you to work here to pay off your room and board once you are well. You better get well soon as this place is rather pricey.

"Father got you a set of civilian clothes to wear, which you'll need to reimburse him for as well. We couldn't have you wearing your uniform at Ady's as there are quite a few southern sympathizers staying here and they can get pretty riled up when it comes to politics and southern loyalty."

"Rest assured, I will pay my way just as soon as I can. That includes to you for saving my leg and my life. I was brought up properly and honor my debts and my obligations."

"Oh, don't worry, you don't owe me anything. I want to do my part and to contribute any way that I can. Of course, I don't know if saving the life of a deserter is considered contributing, but you got to take what you can get."

"I am not a deserter. I was lost and confused and once I have my thoughts about me, I will report back to my unit. I am not afraid, but I do think that I might not have the conscience to continue this fight. If I can serve my country in some other manner, I will. The killing is so senseless and horrific. I don't want to be a part of it anymore."

"I can understand that, Robert, but I'm not sure the Army will feel the same way as you. They might shoot you on sight. Do they still do that?"

"Nope! Word is that President Lincoln called a halt to it because the impression was that we were killing as many of our men as the enemy. Seems that it was hurting morale or some such thing.

"I need to get dressed and find your father and thank him for helping me and for allowing you to care for me."

"Well, you are not going anywhere for a couple more days. That hunk of metal has only been gone for four days and you need to stay off your feet for another two. I will find you a crutch and we'll work on your walking in a day or so. Until then, bed for you, Private Edwards!"

"So, Mindy, just so I make certain I understand. You'll help me get back on my feet again and then I'm on my own. No more caregiving. No more consoling. No more you. Strange, I know, but I think I feel a relapse coming on."

"Why, Robert, are you flirting with your nurse? You are a soldier, aren't you? I'll tell you what, you get well and we can discuss things later. You know, you have a bad leg and I love to dance! Probably wouldn't work."

She hustled off and Robert was left to stare. He did.

14: Farnsworth's Charge

On the hot evening of July 3, 1863, the last battle of Gettysburg, to become known historically as *Farnsworth's Charge*, took place. The Union Army's youngest General (one day younger than Custer), Elon Farnsworth received five wounds (each would have been fatal) in the ill-fated charge and died in the field. Captain Harris, who recruited Hiram and Robert, died that night from wounds received. First Lieutenant Sidney Knowles, the Regimental Adjutant, was killed by a musket ball to the head while attempting to jump a wall at a full gallop. Hiram was shot in the left elbow, resulting in surgery the next morning to remove his arm. Having been shot early in the charge, Hiram witnessed the death of Sidney Knowles.

Many questioned the sanity of such a charge. The

necessity was also in deep doubt. However, it did send the clear message that the battle of Gettysburg was over and that General Robert E. Lee had lost. From this battle on this day, the 1st West Virginia Cavalry began to build the reputation of being one of the best of the US Army's cavalry units. However, it would prove to be Hiram's last battle with Company E.

Hiram wrote to his father...

Hanover, Pa. July 12, 1863

Dear Father: I was assured that you were notified of my injury at Gettysburg. Know that I am recovering quickly and will be returning to my company soon. I have concerns that the loss of my arm may bring my active participation in this war to an end, but I am willing to stay if allowed.

Things have been happening quickly since we were reorganized in Frederick City and General Kilpatrick assumed command of the Division. On the 29th of June, we left Frederick and met the enemy at Hanover, Pennsylvania the next day. We routed the enemy cavalry but lost 2 men and suffered other losses as some of our men were taken prisoner.

For the first two days of July we scouted the area and reported enemy movements as best we could. On the 3rd, we moved closer to Gettysburg and ended up leading a charge under the command of General Farnsworth and led by our Colonel Richmond. To say that this charge was made under the worst of circumstances would be minimizing the difficulties we faced. After moving through heavy woods, we charged over broken ground with boulders, stone and rail fences everywhere in our path. The enemy could not be better protected than they were and to say the attack was chaos does not do the events justice. I have never been as excited before nor after as when they sounded that charge.

Captain Harris was mortally injured and Lt. Knowles was killed almost immediately. I saw Sidney fall, shot through the head. Before that, I felt this instant and terrific pain and realized that I had been shot. I did not know the severity of the wound because as quickly as it came, the pain was gone. I knew almost immediately that my left hand was not grasping the reins and the horse was running free. I holstered my pistol and struggled to get Tater under control. At that time, Colonel Richmond and our troops jumped their horses over the stone wall and were immediately out of sight. I was close to losing consciousness, turned Tater and left the field. I learned that we lost General Farnsworth in the ensuing second wave. He was a very popular officer, although not as flamboyant as Custer.

I was out of the battle upon return to the command and transported at some point by ambulance to Hanover. Doctor Capehart took care of my wounded left arm the morning of the 4th. I don't know if that was done in a field unit or at the Hanover hospital. I don't remember much so I must have lost consciousness early in the operation, but I do remember a lot of pain. There is still quite a bit, but the Colonel says that the arm is healing nicely, wherever it is.

I have been tasked to write Mrs. Knowles concerning her husband, so I will end this for now. Hoping that this letter finds you and the family well and helps to ease any concerns you may have for me. I will be fine and remain your loving son,

Hiram.

Hiram wrote the following letter to Susan Knowles, once he had recovered adequately to do so. Mrs. Knowles provided the letter to the local paper, *The Athens Messenger...*

Death of Lieut. Knowles, of the First Va. Cavalry.

The following sad letter was handed us for publication, but was unavoidably crowed out last week:

Hanover, Pa., July 31, 1863.

Mrs. Knowles: You have no doubt heard of the death of your husband before this time, but I shall endeavor to give you a few of the particulars that perhaps may be of some satisfaction to you. On the 3rd inst., we were engaged with the enemy pretty near all day trying to ascertain their position as near as possible. As I have before stated we were skirmishing all day until about five o'clock in the evening when the Rebel Infantry commenced driving in our skirmishes, consequently a charge was ordered immediately by our Division Command General Kilpatrick. It was a very difficult place for Cavalry to engage the enemy with any prospect of success, but, of course, all we had to do, was to obey orders and go ahead which we did without hesitation. We moved forward cautiously until arriving near where the rebels were in position, and then dashed on them; but they were fortified behind stone-fences, so that their position was almost impenetrable, but their regiment charged over the fence into the rebel ranks and Just as Lieut. Knowles was crossing the fence, he was shot directly through the head, killing him instantly, but he did not fall alone, there were several of our best and bravest officers fell in the same charge.

Mrs. Knowles: It is very hard to have one separated for life that is so dear; but he fell nobly following his Colonel and leading his regiment in defense of our glorious but now bleeding nation.

It will be a consolation to you, for to know that you had a husband, who was not to be excelled as an officer, and there never was a braver man drew a sword in the defense of his country than he was. He was beloved and respected by all who knew him, especially, by the men and officers of the First Virginia Cavalry.

If I had not met with such a misfortune at the time of his death, I should have made every effort possible to have his remains sent home, by express, but I was wounded so severely myself that I could not attend to anything at that time.

Dr. Garden, The Surgeon of our Regiment requests me to say to you that he saw an agent from Washington City, who attends to collecting all back pay and claims of deceased officers and soldiers, and the address of companion and friends, who may receive such claims. And that he (the Doctor) gave him Lt. Knowles' name and your P. O. address. He will perhaps send you the proper papers before long for your signature and perusal.

I think that he is a man who is perfectly acquainted with the business of his profession and that the matter will be perfectly safe entrusted in his care. I think that I shall give him the collection of my accounts such as back pay bounty and pension.

I should have written you before this, but my circumstances have been such that it was impossible to do so. Hoping that my few remarks may be satisfactory and acceptable. I have the honor to be

Yours, with respect,
HIRAM ROBINETT,
Lieut. 1st Va. Cavalry

Death of Lieut. Knowles, of the First Va. Cavalry.

The following sad letter was handed us for publication, but was unavoidably crowded out last week:

HANOVER, PA., July 31st, 1863.

Mrs. Knowles: You have no doubt heard of the death of your husband before this time, but I shall endeavor to give you a few of the particulars, that perhaps may be of some satisfaction to you. On the 3d inst., we were engaged with the enemy pretty near all day trying to ascertain their position as near as possible. As I have before stated we were skirmishing all day until about five o'clock in the evening when the Rebel Infantry commenced driving in our skirmishes, consequently a charge was ordered immediately by our Division Commander General Kilpatrick. It was a very difficult place for Cavalry to engage the enemy with any prospect of success, but, of course, all we had to do, was to obey orders and go ahead which we did without hesitation. We moved forward cautiously until arriving near where the rebels were in position, and then dashed on them; but they were fortified behind stone-fences, so that their position was almost impenetrable, but their regiment charged over the fence into the rebel ranks and just as Lieut. Knowles was crossing the fence, he was shot directly through the head, killing him instantly, but he did not fall alone, there were several of our best and bravest officers fell in the same charge.

MRS. KNOWLES: It is very hard to have one separated for life that is so dear; but he fell nobly following his Colonel and leading his regiment in defence of our glorious but now bleeding country.

The Athens Messenger Archive, Ohio University Library

It will be a consolation to you, for to know that you had a husband, who was no[illegible] excelled as an officer, and there n[illegible] a braver man drew a sword in th[illegible] of his country than he was. He was beloved and respected by all who knew him, especially, by the men and officers of the First Virginia Cavalry.

If I had not met with such a misfortune at the time of his death, I should have made every effort possible to had his remains sent home, by express, but I was wounded so severely myself that I could not attend to anything at that time.

Dr. Gardner, The Surgeon of our Regiment requests me to say to you that he saw an agent from Washington City, who attends to collecting all back pay and claims of deceased officers and soldiers, and the address of companions and friends, who may receive such claims. And that he (the Doctor) gave him Lt. Knowles' name and your P. O. address. He will perhaps send you the proper papers before long for your signature and perusal.

I think that he is a man who is perfectly acquainted with the business of his profession and that the matter will be perfectly safe entrusted in his care. I think that I shall give him the collection of my accounts such as back pay bounty and pensions.

I should have written you before this, but my circumstances have been such that it was impossible to do so.

Hoping that my few remarks may be satisfactory and acceptable. I have the honor to be

Yours, with respect.
HIRAM ROBINETT.
Lieut. 1st Va. Cavalry.

The Athens Messenger Archive, Ohio University Library

15: Hiram Promoted but Prepares to Resign

Hiram reported back to his company in August 1863 near Gainesville, Virginia. He received word that he was to be promoted to 1st Lieutenant but could not muster because of his injury. Instead, he began the disheartening effort to resign his commission as he was deemed unfit to perform his duties because of the loss of his arm.

Ezekiel responded to Hiram's letter...

Company E, 1st West Virginia Cavalry
Stanton, Virginia
1 August 1863

Lt. Hiram Robinett

Dear Son,

Thank you for your letter describing your challenges as Gettysburg. As you might expect, I was extremely upset when I was notified of your injury and I was quite afraid as well. Your letter helped assure me that you are going to make it through this horrific experience. I continue to be amazed at your strength and maturity. I am not certain that I would handle events as well as you continue to do. Without getting totally emotional, I hope you know how proud your family is of you and what you are doing for our country.

To bring you up to date in local news, we had our own excitement about the time you were facing impossible odds in battle. Rebel cavalry troops led by General Morgan came to Nelsonville on Monday, July 20th. Everyone had been warned but no one knew where or when they would show up, so it was difficult to be prepared.

The only advance precaution that I could take was to bury our valuables in the grove, out of sight of the house but reasonably safe. We planned, if given enough notice, to take the horse and cow into the woods and hope for the best. As it turns out, while they were throughout the area, they never came to Chauncey or near our farm.

Andrew had the most exciting experience. The canal and the boats in Nelsonville were a target and Andrew said 10 boats were destroyed by fire. He saw most of the canal action occur and was surprised how business-like the rebels were. They didn't harm anyone, did what they came to do, took all the good horses and departed. The Rebs set fire to the bridge crossing the Hocking but Andrew and the citizens put it out before any damage was done. Morgan camped overnight in Buchtel and apparently left there without doing much damage.

Union General Shackleford was hot on Morgan's trail and arrived in Nelsonville 4 hours behind the Rebs. The citizens were very happy to see the Union soldiers and prepared a feast for them. With the Rebs just over the hill in Buchtel, it seems that Shackleford lost a good opportunity to capture them, but his troops had ridden hard and were apparently worn out. They feasted, rested and the next morning traveled on to Buchtel to find that the Rebs had departed during the night.

Things have settled back to normal around here. It's been hot and not a lot of rain, so the corn looks bad right now. We have had a good garden and the girls have been canning quite a bit already. If we get some rain in the next week or so, we should be fine. The boys are putting in hay for the stock and orders are keeping me busy with salt barrels.

Mother is fine and worries about you almost as much as I do. If you get a chance, drop her a note. It would surprise her and mean a lot to her as well. Until next time, write and stay safe.

Your father,
Ezekiel
Chauncey Road, Chauncey
Athens County, Ohio, USA

16: Meanwhile, Back in Towson, Maryland

Apparently, time flies when you're a deserter. Before Robert knew it, it was the middle of August and he had just recently tossed the crutches aside. He still suffered a slight limp and occasionally was using a cane for some relief. He was getting stronger each day but wasn't certain that he could ever be a horse soldier again. Of course, he wasn't thinking that he wanted to be one either. He knew that each day away from his regiment was digging the hole he found himself in deeper and it was slowly filling with slippery mud. The day would arrive that he would have to figure a way out of this trouble but for now, he had to heal and pay back this debt that he found himself accumulating each day.

Having talked with the Hotel Manager, Robert had convinced him that he would be a capable handyman.

Explaining that his father was a cabinet maker and craftsman and that he had learned multiple skills assisting him, the manager decided to give him a try. So far, it was working out well in Robert's estimation and he felt the manager would agree.

Most days the hours were long and busy. The work was rarely difficult and there had been no major projects undertaken. These results did give Robert time to get to know Towson town and he had gone into Baltimore several times. He had to be careful because he felt like he stood out and he didn't want to be noticed until he could work this desertion problem out on his own. He wasn't exactly certain how he might do that yet, but would keep looking for the answer.

On September 1st, an event occurred that would have a significant impact on Robert's immediate future. It appeared minimal at the time and only later would its importance become obvious.

Descending to the lobby from the second floor, Robert noticed a small congregation of new arrivals apparently checking in. A middle-aged gentleman, very neatly attired was talking with the Hotel Manager. The man was accompanied by a young woman, equally decked-out. Surveying her, Robert decided that while she was not beautiful, she carried herself very well and was quite attractive. Long curls of black hair braided over her shoulders and framed a face that certainly would grow on you with more frequent appraisals. She possessed a prominent nose that seemed to enhance the mystery in her eyes, which were pretty. While not in any way like Melinda Booth, Robert found a definite attraction to this new arrival. No Mindy Booth but nice still the same.

Robert needed to report his progress to the manager and attempted to stand aside and wait patiently. To his utter amazement, the aristocratic traveler took notice of the handyman and turned to him with a gorgeous smile. Robert was significantly impressed when she obviously overlooked his menial status and spoke to him.

"Hi, how are you today?" Her question seemed genuine. Robert knew that he didn't stumble with his reply, but he felt as if he were talking in slow motion.

"I'm fine. How are you? Welcome to Ady's. Is this your first stay with us?" Robert noticed the Manager watching him and found himself thinking cleaning the stables would be his next assignment. Hey, he didn't start this conversation with a guest, the guest did. He was just a friendly employee welcoming her to Ady's.

She introduced herself as Miss. Belle Boyd[7] from Martinsburg, Virginia. She was accompanying her aunt's business manager to Baltimore. She offered that her aunt owned and operated a hotel in Front Royal. She spoke of the difficulties of keeping the hotel adequately supplied with the war going on. She talked as if the war was merely an inconvenience and Robert surmised that was likely the case for a lady of her stature.

Belle, who had graduated from the prestigious Mount Washington Female College in Baltimore, was curious as to what Robert was doing in Towson and why he wasn't in the fight.

While forgetting to mention the desertion situation, Robert did share that he was a battle injured soldier and was taking time to recover before returning to the fray.

Belle's companion had completed the check-in process and the bell hop had the bags ready to deliver, so Belle bid Robert a more than casual farewell with the suggestion that she might see him later. As the party departed, Robert found himself hoping that might be the case. The Manager, clearing his throat abruptly, brought Robert back to earth.

The next day, Wednesday, was uneventful for Robert. On Thursday morning, he was given the task to check the bed in Room 316. Told only that it needed repair, Robert carried the essentials with him. Knocking for entry, he was shocked when Belle Boyd answered the knock. The immediate thought was that in just two days, she had become more attractive. She wore what appeared to be a dressing gown and the soft blue of the gown increased the intensity of her eyes. What wonderful eyes. Her smile showed brilliantly white teeth and Robert knew immediately that it would be okay if she wanted to bite him. He was very certain that he had never experienced a feeling such as this in his short lifetime. Mindy Booth popped into his mind and the quick comparison was made. Mindy had far more natural beauty, there was no comparison there. However, Belle radiated something Robert had never experienced before. It finally dawned on him. It was sex.

Making a feeble attempt to regain some semblance of self-control, Robert mumbled something about looking at her bed. She stepped back to allow him to enter, but immediately stepped forward again and closed the gap between them. This bold maneuver caused Robert to brush up against her soft body and he immediately had a new goal in life. It was Belle Boyd.

Of course, with his limited experience in the arena of sexual encounters, he had no idea what would come next. Fortunately for Robert, Belle apparently was more experienced in this area and she took control. Circling his neck with her long sensuous arms, she raised her lips to his and kissed him lightly, then growing stronger by the second. She tasted good, almost sweet, warm. Tugging at him without lessening her grip, they made the trip entwined to the bed.

Robert again mumbled, "Are you certain this is alright? Don't you want me to check the bed?"

Belle replied amusingly, "That's what we are doing and that is why I asked specifically for you, Robert!"

What else could he do? Robert began to seriously check the bed. He checked it for softness, firmness, warmness, and every other *ness* he could think of. At some point in the heat of the moment, Belle urgently moaned, "Don't stop, don't stop!"

Stopping was the furthest thing in his mind, in fact, it had never entered his mind. At the height of his passion, Robert erupted and experienced his first shared orgasm. Belle, equally excited, asked, "You're not done, are you?" Robert responded, "I don't know, I've never done this before!" Belle giggled almost like a child and replied, "Well, then, trust me. You're not done!" Robert was very happy to hear that.

At some point in the day, they had to stop. There was virtually nothing left to try. The race had been run, the horse was spent and back in the barn and the jockey was exhausted.

They lay in the bed, which obviously was not broken. It had withstood the most strenuous test Robert could muster. They talked, mostly about Robert and his experience with the First Virginia Cavalry. He failed again to mention desertion, but he babbled about every other detail he knew, probably bragging somewhat but Belle appeared genuinely interested. She seemed to care about his adventures. Of course, being only a Private, Robert could not offer much for any of the more in-depth questions that she asked. Having been the clerk for General Stahel seemed of great interest to her, as were the orders and reports Robert had transcribed for the General.

When Robert finally left Belle's room, he decided that this had been one of the more enjoyable mornings ever. He thought that he would like to do that again in a day or so. He considered turning around and returning now. First, he had to report back to the Manager that the bed in 316 had been examined thoroughly and was not in need of repair. He did take care of a few issues to the apparent satisfaction of the guest. She seemed to be happy. When the Manager smiled, and thanked him, Robert wanted to laugh but thought better of it.

There were no requests for service from 316 on Friday, much to Robert's disappointment. Early Saturday morning, he ascended the stairs to the 3rd floor and immediately noticed the door to 316 open and a maid's cart close by. Entering the room, he was surprised to hear that the occupant had checked out abruptly last evening. Checking at the front desk, hoping for a message or a note, there was none. He was informed that Miss. Boyd had departed in the escort of several Union soldiers. Robert was disappointed but upon reflection, not surprised. He guessed his bed checking career had come to an end.

The heat of summer turned to the chill of fall and Robert continued to work and wonder. The work was never hard but it was steady and he enjoyed the environment. He could see himself in the hotel business but would prefer being an owner or manager over a handy-man position. Robert continued to ponder how he was going to resolve his military issue, but he was busy enough to justify in his mind putting it off. However, there are some situations where the interests of others outweigh your own personal situation. This proved to be one of those times.

17: Hiram Applies and is Discharged

Surgeons Certificate of Disability

Medical Department 1st Va. Cav

Near Gainesville Virginia

October 25, 1863

Lieutenant Hiram Robinett of 1st Virginia Mounted Volunteers having applied for a certificate on which to ground an application to resign his commission as 2nd Lieutenant Co E, 1st Virginia Cavalry:

I certify that I have this day carefully examined this officer and find that on the 3rd day of July A.D. 1863, while in action at Gettysburg, Pennsylvania, he received a gunshot wound in the left arm rendering amputation necessary and that said operation was performed by Surgeon Capehart on the 4th day of July A.D. 1863, thereby wholly disqualifying the said

Hiram Robinett for the duties of an officer in Cavalry – And hereby recommend that his resignation be accepted.

P. Gardner Asst & Actg Surg, 1st Va Cav

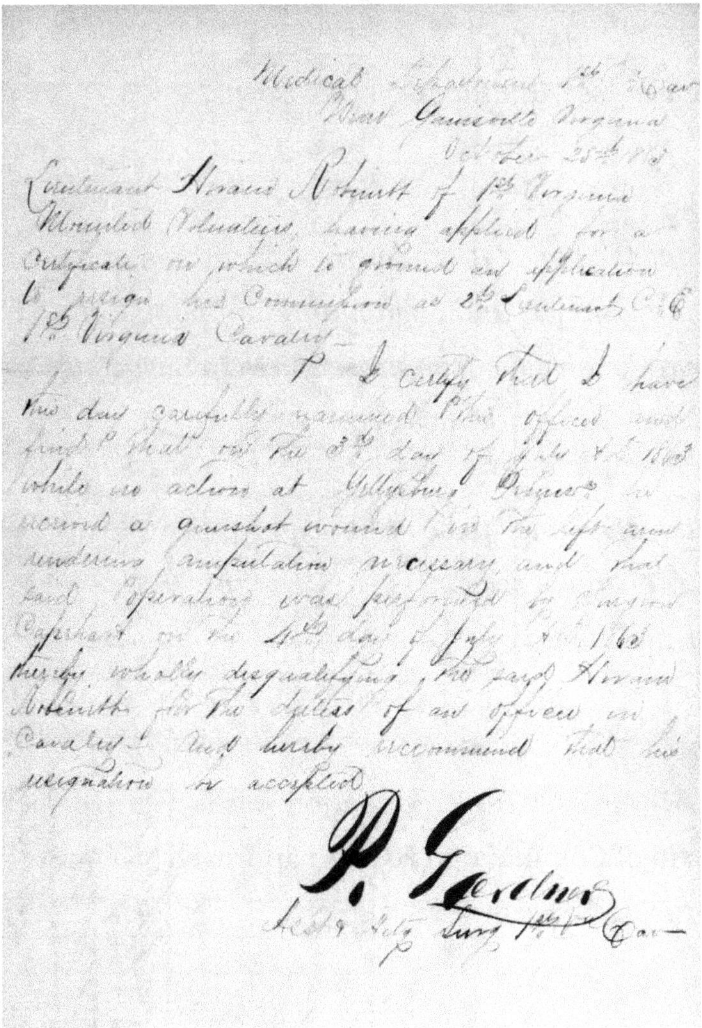

Medical Department 1st Va Cav
Near Gainesville Virginia
October 25th 1863

Lieutenant Hiram Robinett of 1st Virginia Mounted Volunteers, having applied for a Certificate on which to ground an application to resign his Commission as 2nd Lieutenant Co. E 1st Virginia Cavalry.

I do certify that I have this day carefully examined this officer and find that on the 3rd day of July A.D. 1863 while in action at Gettysburg Pennsylvania he received a gunshot wound in the left arm rendering amputation necessary and that said operation was performed by Surgeon Capehart on the 4th day of July A.D. 1863 thereby wholly disqualifying the said Hiram Robinett for the duties of an officer in Cavalry. And hereby recommend that his resignation be accepted.

P. Gardner
Asst & Actg Surg 1st Va Cav

Surgeons Certificate of Disability. Source: www.archives.gov

Letter of Resignation

Camp 1st Virginia Cavalry
Near Gainesville Virginia
October 28, 1863

To: C.C. Snydaur
Capt & Asst Adjutant Gen Cav Corps,

Sir,
I have the honor to tender the resignation of my Commission as 2nd Lieutenant, Company E, 1st Virginia Cavalry on grounds set forth in Surgeons Certificate - herewith enclosed.

I have the honor to be very respectfully
Your obedient servant.
Hiram Robinett

Hiram's letter of resignation was forwarded via the Chain of Command to HQ and approved. S.O. 189 Cav Corps, effective Oct. 28, 1863.

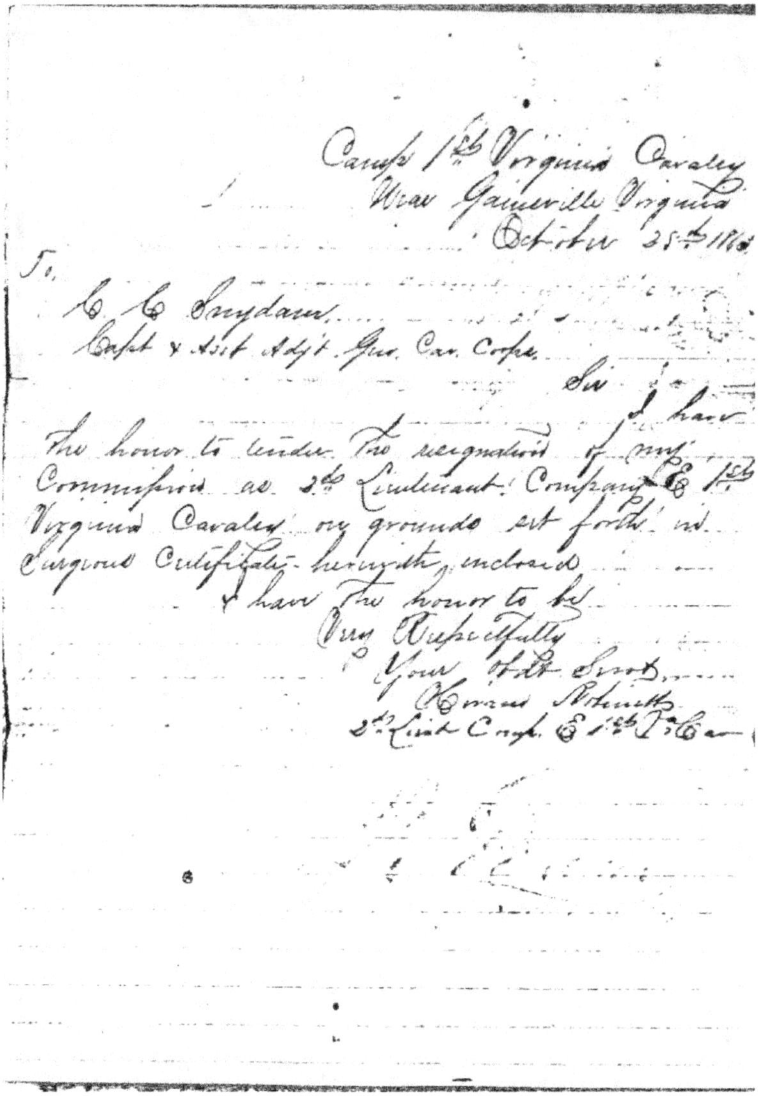

Camp 1st Virginia Cavalry
Near Gainesville Virginia
October 25th 186[illegible]

To,
C. C. Suydam
Capt & Asst Adjt. Gen. Cav. Corps.

Sir I have the honor to tender the resignation of my Commission as 2d Lieutenant Company E 1st Virginia Cavalry on grounds set forth in Surgeons Certificate herewith enclosed.

I have the honor to be
Very Respectfully
Your Obdt Servt,
Horace Robinett
2d Lieut Comp. E 1st V. Cav

Letter of Resignation   Source: www.archives.gov

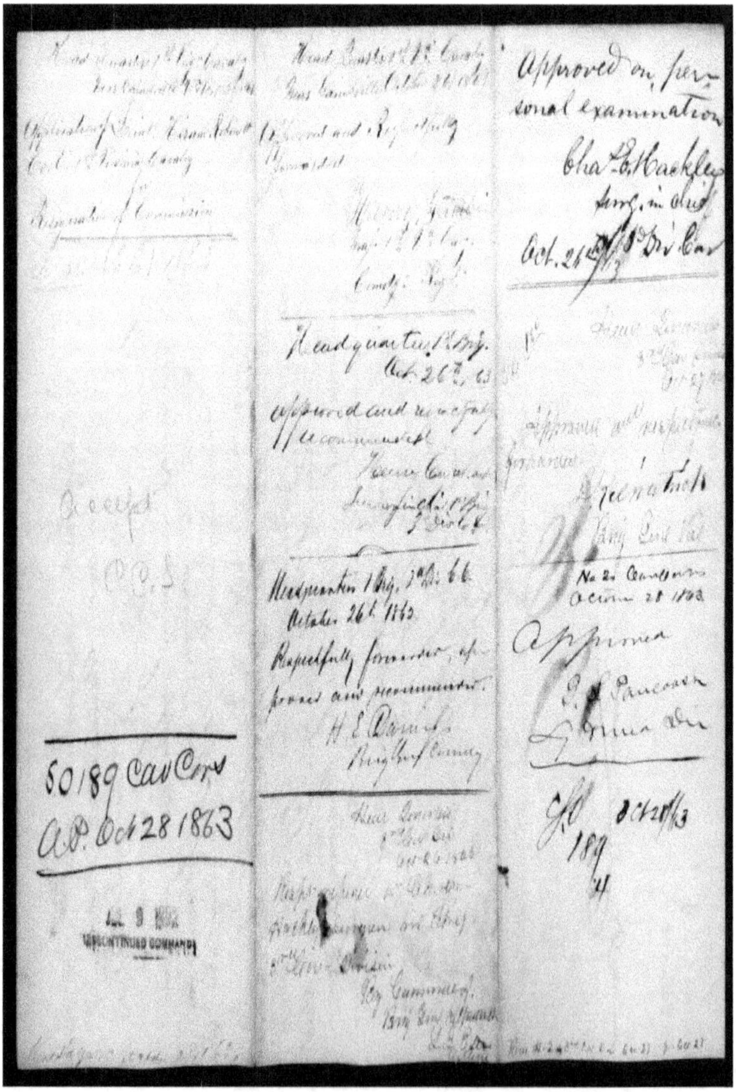
Approved on personal examination
Oct. 26th/63

Headquarters 1st Brig.
Oct. 26th, 63

October 26th 1863
Respectfully forwarded, approved and recommended.

50189 Cav Corps
A.P. Oct 28 1863

Resignation Approval. Source: www.archives.gov

18: HIRAM, THE CIVILIAN

Upon Hiram's discharge from the 1st West Virginia Cavalry in late October 1863, he remained in Washington D.C. He acquired a room at Mrs. Brannon's Boarding House at 447 Pennsylvania Avenue. Hiram had met Mrs. Brannon at Cliffburne Army Hospital, where he was receiving treatment for his left elbow. It was healing well but occasionally had some minor issues that required attending.

Taking the same advice that he had offered to Mrs. Knowles, Hiram filed for his Invalid Army Pension through the law firm of Stewart, Stevens and Company. Colonel N. P. Richmond and Lieutenant Leasure vouched for Hiram's identity and the Colonel also provided a statement as to the events leading to Hiram's disabling injury at the Battle of Gettysburg. This would turn out to be a long drawn out process and Hiram and many others would not receive pension compensation for almost two years. However, when finally approved and initial payment was made, it was from the date of discharge.

Form for Declaration for an Invalid Army Pension

State of District of Columbia
County of Washington

On this 4th day of November one thousand eight hundred and sixty three, personally appeared before me, a Justice of the Peace, within and for the county and State aforesaid, Hiram Robinett, aged 21 years, a resident of Chauncey, Athens Co, in the State of Ohio, who, being duly sworn according to law, declares that he is the identical Hiram Robinett who enlisted in the service of the United States at Clarksburg, Va., on the 4th day of January, in the year 1862, as a Private in Company E, commanded by Captain William W Harris, in the 1st regiment of the Virginia Cavalry, in the War of 1861, and was honorably promoted to a 2nd Lieutenant on the 18th of January 1863, and was hon-

orably discharged on the 28th day of October, in the year 1863 by Special Order No. 189; that while in the service aforesaid, and in the line of his duty, he received the following disability: While engaged in a cavalry charge at the battle of Gettysburg, on the 3rd July, 1863, he received a gunshot wound through the elbow joint of the left arm causing amputation necessary; which was performed on the morning of July 4th following. He further declares that he was commissioned as a 1st Lieutenant on the 12th of August following but was not mustered into service on account of the loss of his arm as aforesaid - and that his post office address is Chauncey, Athens Co., Ohio - and I hereby authorize Stewart, Stevens & Co, of the City of Washington, D.C., to procure for me the Pension which I may be found entitled to under the Act of Congress, approved July 14, 1862, and to receive and receipt for any certificate which may issue in my favor in connection with the above application.

Hiram Robinette

Also, personally appeared N.P. Richmond of Indianapolis and Henry J. Leasure, resident of Wheeling, Western Virginia, persons who I certify to be respectable, and entitled to credit, and who by me being duly sworn, say that they were present and saw Hiram Robinett sign his name (or make his mark) to the foregoing declaration,

N. P. Richmond Col. 1st Va Cav
Henry J. Leasure Lieut 1st Va Cav

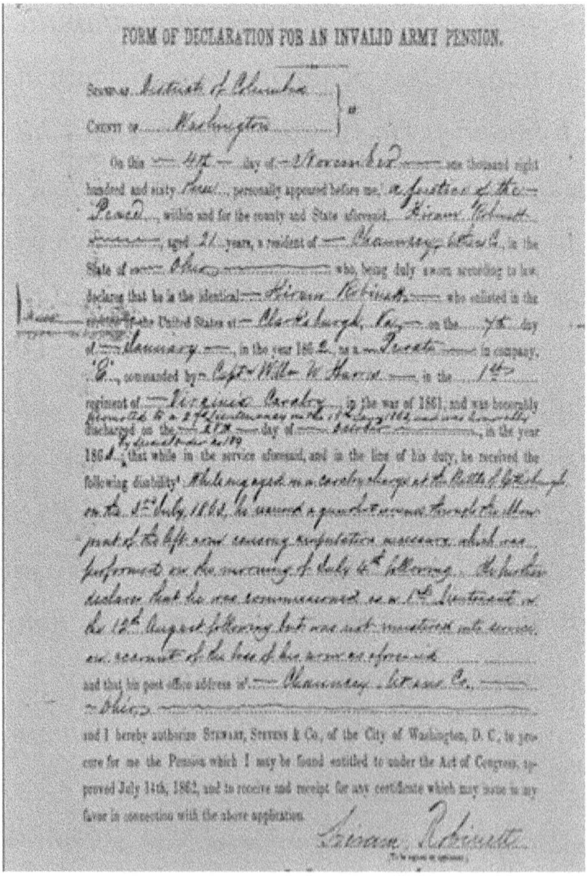

FORM OF DECLARATION FOR AN INVALID ARMY PENSION.

State of District of Columbia
County of Washington } ss

On this 4th day of November one thousand eight hundred and sixty three, personally appeared before me, a Justice of the Peace, within and for the county and State aforesaid, Hiram Robinett, aged 21 years, a resident of Chauncey [illegible], in the State of Ohio who, being duly sworn according to law, declares that he is the identical Hiram Robinett who enlisted in the service of the United States at Clarksburgh, Va on the 7th day of January, in the year 1862, as a Private in company "E", commanded by Capt. Wm W. Harris, in the 1st regiment of Virginia Cavalry, in the war of 1861, and was honorably [illegible] discharged on the [illegible] day of [illegible], in the year 186[illegible]; that while in the service aforesaid, and in the line of his duty, he received the following disability: While engaged in a cavalry charge at the Battle of Gettysburgh on the 3rd July 1863, he received a gunshot wound through the elbow joint of the left arm causing amputation necessary which was performed on the morning of July 4th following. He further declares that he was commissioned as a 1st Lieutenant on the 12th August following but was not mustered into service on account of the loss of his arm as aforesaid

and that his post office address is Chauncey [illegible] Co. Ohio

and I hereby authorize Stewart, Stevens & Co., of the City of Washington, D. C., to procure for me the Pension which I may be found entitled to under the Act of Congress, approved July 14th, 1862, and to receive and receipt for any certificate which may issue in my favor in connection with the above application.

Hiram Robinett

Invalid Army Pension. Source: www.archives.gov

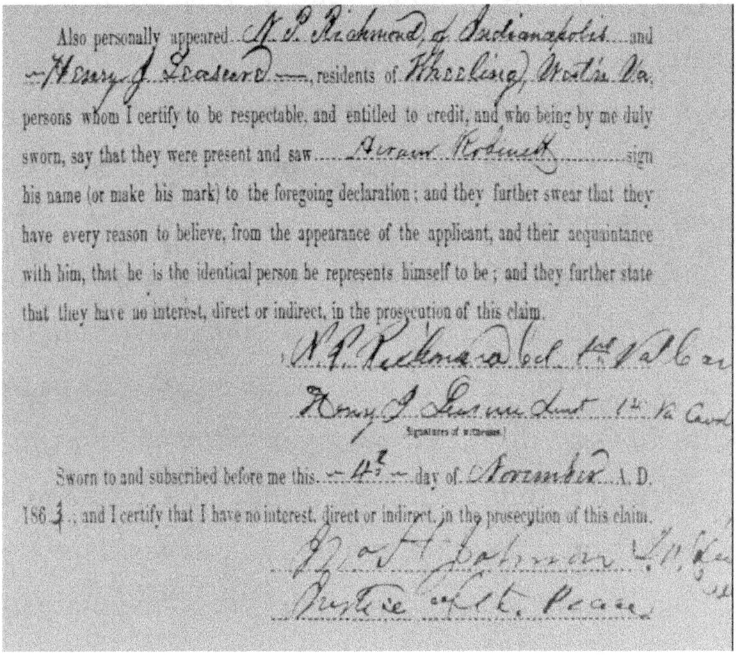

Also personally appeared N. P. Richmond, of Indianapolis and Henry J. Seasard, residents of Wheeling, West Va., persons whom I certify to be respectable, and entitled to credit, and who being by me duly sworn, say that they were present and saw Aaron Rodneck sign his name (or make his mark) to the foregoing declaration; and they further swear that they have every reason to believe, from the appearance of the applicant, and their acquaintance with him, that he is the identical person he represents himself to be; and they further state that they have no interest, direct or indirect, in the prosecution of this claim.

N. P. Richmond Col 1st Va Cav

Henry J. Seasard Lieut 1st Va Cavl

(Signatures of witnesses.)

Sworn to and subscribed before me this 4th day of November A. D. 1863, and I certify that I have no interest, direct or indirect, in the prosecution of this claim.

Robt H Johnson J. P.

Justice of the Peace

Invalid Army Pension 2. Source: www.archives.gov

Certificate of Disability

I certify that 2nd Lieut. Hiram Robinett, of Captain Wm. N. Harris' Company E of the 1st Regiment of Virginia Volunteer Cavalry was enlisted by Capt. Harris of the 1st Regiment of the Va. Vol Cav at Clarksburg, on the 7th day of January 1863, to serve 3 years (or during the War.) He was born in Waterloo in the State of Ohio, is 21 years of age; 5 feet 10 inches high; dark complexion; grey eyes; black hair; and by occupation, when enlisted, a Farmer.

I further certify that I personally know of the following facts and circumstances connected with his disability: While engaged in a Cavalry charge at the Battle of Gettysburg, Pa, on the 3rd day of July 1863, he received a gunshot wound through the elbow joint of the left-arm, causing amputation, which was performed on the morning of July 4th, following. The wound aforesaid was received in line of duty, and while nobly battling for the flag of his country.

N. P. Richmond
Col. 1st Va. Vol. Cav.

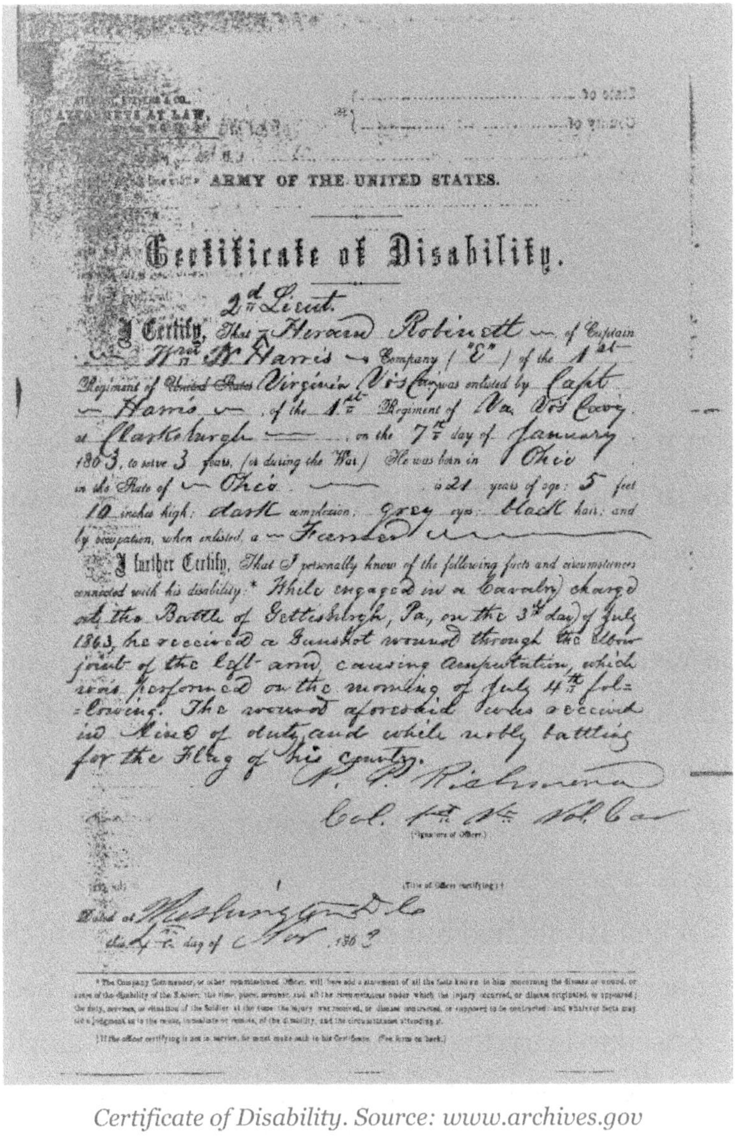

ARMY OF THE UNITED STATES.

Certificate of Disability.

2d Lieut.

I Certify, That Hiram Robinett of Captain Wm. H. Harris Company ("E") of the 1st Regiment of ~~United States~~ Virginia Vol Cavy was enlisted by Capt Harris of the 1st Regiment of Va. Vol Cavy at Clarksburgh on the 7th day of January 1863, to serve 3 years (or during the War.) He was born in Ohio in the State of Ohio, is 21 years of age; 5 feet 10 inches high; dark complexion; grey eyes; black hair; and by occupation, when enlisted, a Farmer.

I further Certify, That I personally know of the following facts and circumstances connected with his disability:* While engaged in a Cavalry charge at the Battle of Gettysburgh, Pa, on the 3d day of July 1863, he received a Gunshot wound through the Elbow joint of the left arm, causing amputation, which was performed on the morning of July 4th following. The wound aforesaid was received in line of duty and while nobly battling for the Flag of his country.

[illegible]
Col. 1st Va Vol. Cav
(Signature of Officer.)

(Title of Officer certifying.)†

Dated at Washington D.C.
this [illegible] day of Nov 1863

* The Company Commander, or other commissioned Officer, will here add a statement of all the facts known to him concerning the disease or wound, or cause of the disability of the Soldier; the time, place, manner, and all the circumstances under which the injury occurred, or disease originated or appeared; the duty, service, or situation of the Soldier at the time the injury was received, or disease contracted, or supposed to be contracted; and whatever facts may aid a judgment as to the cause, importance or extent, of the disability, and the circumstances attending it.

† If the officer certifying is not in service, he must make oath to his Certificate. (See form on back.)

Certificate of Disability. Source: www.archives.gov

19: What's Next

Hiram had saved enough of his Army pay that allowed him to remain in Washington and decide what he was going to do, now that he was unemployed. He was aware that he might have the opportunity to re-up in the Veteran Reserve Corps and this was a strong consideration if he could retain his current rank of 2nd Lieutenant or perhaps pick up the promotion that he had earned but was unable to muster for because of his injury.

When Hiram had returned to his company from the recuperation stay at Hanover Hospital, he had been surprised to learn that Robert Edwards was missing in action. More surprising was that it looked more and more like desertion, several days after the Gettysburg battle. Hiram knew Robert was a free spirit, but also knew he was not a coward or a traitor, so it was quite the mystery. Hiram was staying in touch with friends in his former unit and knew that Robert's location was still unknown in mid-November. Hiram decided that President Lincoln's *Day of Thanksgiving* would be the best time to visit Chauncey, Hiram hoped he would be able to provide some word on their son to William and Sophronia Edwards. Presently, that looked doubtful.

As it appeared that the next opportunity to go back on active service would be after the new year, Hiram made his plans to travel to Ohio. He mailed a letter to his father and boarded the train mid-morning, 20 November, headed for Marietta, Ohio. He found himself excited to get home and wondered what their reactions might be to his new appearance, missing a hand. He felt the hand was all that was missing as he had become quite adept at using his shortened limb in managing his day to day activities. He often mused that it was difficult to pick his left nostril but that with stubborn persistence, he had learned to cope.

The train trip was uneventful, which was not always the case during war, and was quite invigorating. The cars were crowded, lots of active and ex-military men trying to make it to their destination. Hiram enjoyed some conversation and did not get overly tired explaining his circumstances, figuring it would be good practice for when he got to Chauncey.

From Marietta, there was a scheduled Stage Coach and Hiram paid for an inside seat, which was not always available. On the morning of the 22nd of November, Hiram's coach pulled up in front of the Chauncey Post Office. It had been a relatively quiet trip; the weather was cool and the dust of summer was nowhere to be found. His father was not waiting, which was no surprise, as Hiram figured the letter he mailed might be on this same coach for delivery. He would find a ride easy enough and could surprise all the family at the same time.

The visit was far more enjoyable than he even expected. He got to see all his family and they were in good spirits and reasonable health. Fall and the approach of winter in southern Ohio was Hiram's favorite time of year. The Edwards family came to dinner on Thanksgiving Day and the large crowd was noisy and great fun. Everyone was full of questions and eager for stories and Hiram delighted in recalling his experiences to an excited and well-fed group of loved ones. He certainly didn't have to exaggerate as he had plenty of real-life experiences to share. The most excitement was reserved for Hiram having met General Custer, which surprised Hiram that everyone knew about him. Robert being missing and no one knowing what his story might be was an obvious concern for everyone. Hiram assured Robert's parents that he would immediately pass any information along to them. At dinner, Robert's well-being was the major focus of prayers, along with Curtis and Stineman and the other local boys who were off at war.

Hiram made a trip to visit Susan Knowles which was very sad and uncomfortable for them both. She had two young boys to raise now, on her own.

He stayed another four days and then departed for the Marietta train station. His brother Andrew took him with Moses along for the ride. Hiram was sad that the visit had ended so quickly but he felt he needed to be in Washington to be ready for whatever opportunities might present themselves.

Back in Washington finally, Hiram decided that while he was waiting for things to happen for him, he would look around and see what he could find out about Robert. He figured he owed Robert at least that much.

20: Back in Towson at Ady's Hotel

Winter was approaching. The weather dipped from cool to cold. On the overcast afternoon of December 18th, a group of four Union soldiers entered the lobby. A 1st Lieutenant, obviously in charge, requested to speak to Robert Edwards, the maintenance man. The bell boy was sent to fetch Robert who was working on the second floor. As they came down the stairs, Robert realized immediately that his adventure as a deserter had come to an end.

As Robert identified himself, Privates stepped to each side of and behind him. The Lieutenant asked him point blank: "Are you the same Robert H. Edwards, Private, 1st West Virginia Cavalry, that has been missing since 2 July of this year?"

"Yes Sir, I am."

"Are you the same Robert H. Edwards who deserted his unit at Gettysburg?"

Again, "Yes sir, I am."

"Private Edwards, you are under arrest for deserting your post and will be turned over to the proper authorities for prosecution."

"I understand and have been expecting you fellows for some time. May I retrieve my belongings?

"No, you may not!" and with that said, Robert was escorted out the front door and it would be the last time he would see Ady's Hotel in Towson, Maryland.

Descriptive List of Deserters Arrested.

E, 1st Cav Va - Robt H. Edwards
Pvt, Co. E, 1st Reg, Va Cav
List dated Dec 18, 1863, and signed by Actg Provost Marshal, 2 District of Maryland.
Deserted:
When: July 4, 1863 *Where:* Gettysburg Pa
Arrested:
When: Dec 18, 1863 *Where:* Towsentown Md
Remarks: Brought in charged with Desertion, his own confession sufficient to convict him of Desertion.
Reward allowed $30.
Endorsement on list shows that the men named
Therein were received at Baltimore
Dec 18, 1863

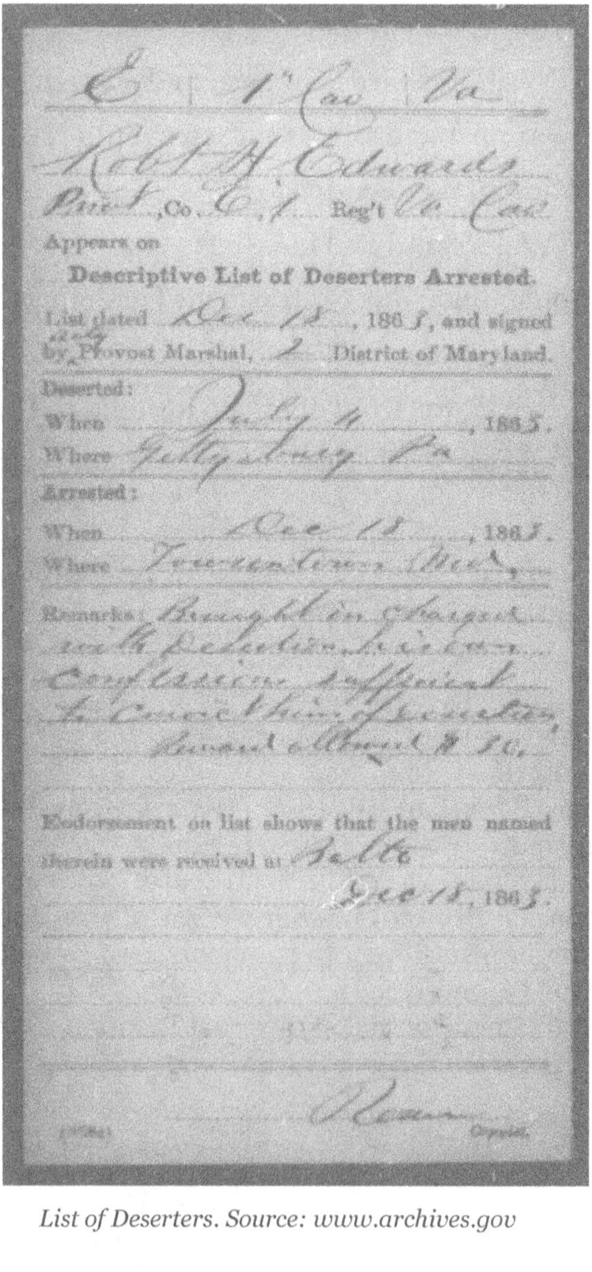

E | 1 Cav | Va

Robt H. Edwards

Prvt, Co. E, 1 Reg't Va Cav

Appears on

Descriptive List of Deserters Arrested.

List dated Dec 18, 1865, and signed by Asst Provost Marshal, 2 District of Maryland.

Deserted:

When July 4, 1863.

Where Gettysburg Pa

Arrested:

When Dec 18, 1865.

Where Towsontown Md

Remarks: Brought in charged with desertion. His own confession sufficient to convict him of desertion. Reward allowed $ 10.

Endorsement on list shows that the men named therein were received at Balto

Dec 18, 1865.

[illegible]

Copyist.

List of Deserters. Source: www.archives.gov

Robert was initially taken to Fort McHenry, which was in the process of becoming known as the 'Baltimore Bastille'. Still overflowing with prisoners taken during the Battle at Gettysburg, it had reached nearly 7,000 inmates before the processing had whittled it down to currently just over 1,000. This was far more than the 300 prisoners typically incarcerated. The fort previously had held numerous Baltimore City officials, including the Mayor, the former Governor, a Congressman from the 4th District, city police officers, commissioners and others. Even the grandson of Francis Scott Key had been a guest here for a period, so it appeared no one was exempt if thought to be disloyal to the Federal Government.

Being a deserter apparently gave Robert a different status compared to a Confederate soldier. He could be a coward without being a threat to the US Government. Within two days, he was transported with more than 20 others to Washington City and incarcerated in the *Old Capitol* prison. While not told any specifics, he assumed that he was brought here because he was a union soldier and not a Rebel.

Robert was in for quite a surprise.

Old Capital Prison, Washington. Source: www.archives.gov

21: The Prisoner has a Visitor

Having lost tract of time, Robert calculated by his best guess that it was Christmas Day, 1863. In the Old Capitol Prison, it was business as usual.

Robert was in a double cell but had no cell mate presently. He was fed a bowl of oats and a cup of water for breakfast. He ached for a cup of coffee but surmised that if this was a sample of meals to come, he needed a way out of here as quickly as possible. Unfortunately, he didn't have a plan in mind and didn't expect things to change very quickly.

Midmorning he received the surprise of his young life. A guard opens his cell door and informs Robert that he has a visitor and the guard leads him down the passageway, through another iron door that Robert made note of, and into the first of what appeared to be three similar rooms. He assumed this was a visitation room but it was more often used for interrogation, which he would experience in the very near future.

Sitting behind a table in the center of the room was a civilian who Robert failed to recognize initially. Making eye contact, Hiram Robinett asked, “What’s up, kid? You don’t know me?”

Hiram had aged in the six months since they last were together. His face was much thinner with the smile lines deeply etched surrounding his mouth. More prominently, Hiram was missing a hand and forearm. Additionally, he didn’t look comfortable in civilian clothing. Robert felt that he was looking as a different fellow than the one that he had grown up with, and indeed he was.

Robert had a million questions and Hiram had a few of his own. Just like it had always been, back to when they used to sneak out of Church after Sunday School, Hiram was in charge. He asks, “What happened to you at Gettysburg? I learned that in late December you were arrested in Towson, Maryland and admitted that you deserted at Gettysburg in July. A bounty of $30 was paid for your capture, so evidently someone had turned you in. You realize that at some point, you will likely be court martialed and dishonorably discharged from the Army. Again, what the hell happened?"

Robert started in telling his story and Hiram didn't interrupt until he had concluded with being arrested and admitting to desertion.

"And every bit of this story is the truth! The hole I found myself in just kept getting deeper and more complicated and I guess I decided to allow someone else to solve it for me. Uncle Sam came through and now I might just be screwed, but if I am, I suspect that I deserve it for not manning up and doing the right thing."

"Well, I talked with the Officer in Charge and he claims he has no idea what is planned for you. Some higher ups, I don't know what that means, want to talk with you after the holidays. Again, the OIC has no idea what about. Do you?"

"I can't imagine. I was arrested at Ady's Hotel in Towson town and that is a known Southern-sympathetic area for certain. Geez, I hope they don't think I've turned or some such thing. I don't support this war any longer but I certainly am not supporting or sympathetic towards the Rebels. Far from it!"

"Did you make friends with anyone? Was anyone

asking a lot of questions about our Unit, our movements, our goals and objectives?"

"No, not really. I was completely away from the military. I had no idea what was going on, where the Cavalry was, there wasn't anything of value that I could tell anyone. Plus, I wasn't advertising that I had deserted. I told anyone who asked that I was on the mend and would be reporting back as soon as I was able to do my job again."

"Well, apparently, someone of importance thinks that you know something, did something, or are involved in something or they wouldn't have brought you here. If they thought you turned, then they would have shuffled you off to the Reb Prison in Baltimore. They brought you here because you have something to offer or at least they think you do. You might want to think really hard about the past six months because if you have nothing that interests them, they will squash you like a horse fly and be gone."

"Well, they're likely going to do that then because I didn't talk to anyone about my job or my unit. I had nothing to tell. Unless they want to know about me losing my virginity in the past six months, there is nothing to tell."

"Well, at least you won't die without something to repent for. How did you hook up with a woman? Did you hire one? Are you dying from a wartime disease?"

"No! I'm fine and it wasn't a Baltimore prostitute. In fact, it was a very prestigious beautiful young southern lady, visiting on business. She was stunning and perhaps has ruined me for life. I don't think I'll ever find another like her in my lifetime. That's what happens when you start at the very top."

Hiram interrupts. "Spare me the details! I don't want to have to go to church Wednesday night. You said she was a Southerner?"

"She was, in fact, from Clarksburg, Western Virginia. I hope to see more of her but I doubt I'll ever find her again. Thinking about it, Belle, that's her name, she did ask me all about my job, my unit, the General that I was working for. She was interested and it seemed like no detail was too minute for her. I told her lots of little things but I didn't and I don't know anything of value. I'm certain that anything I might have told her fell on deaf ears. She was only a young girl, my age and was more interested in what we were doing than the rebellion. There's nothing there. It was the greatest time of my life but of no significance to anyone else, apparently even her. She scurried off the next day without even a goodbye."

Hiram didn't agree. There didn't seem to be anything of significance there but only because Robert had nothing to tell. Stranger things have happened that turned out to be important. There have been female spies before and there would be many more in the future, he was certain. Who else could get a soldier talking, bragging, telling all or even making stuff up for some belly rubbing time. A beautiful, young, willing female or merely any one of the adjectives described attached to a female should do it. Hiram suspected Robert had been duped, for sure.

Regardless, maybe because it was Christmas Day, the guards were in no hurry for Hiram to vacate, so they talked about many things. Hiram gave extensive details of his fight at Gettysburg. He described the impossible mission they were sent on and he talked about their friend, Sidney Knowles. They talked of home, growing up, school, the future if they lived through this war. They even talked about what would happen if the Rebels were successful. If the Rebels were only interested in breaking away from the United States, that might not be so terrible. However, if through victory, they decided that they wanted it all, then the war would certainly begin again and it would be horrendous, more widely disbursed and much more serious. Other countries would pledge allegiance and assistance to one nation or the other and it would be a real fiasco. It was obvious to these two former warriors that the North must win at all costs as this would likely be their last opportunity to do so.

Hiram finally called it a day. He promised Robert that he would stay in touch and Robert committed to the same to the best of his abilities. Not knowing when, if ever, they would meet face to face again, they shook hands, hugged and ended their visit.

22: Interrogation

When you are in a situation where time is open-ended, it becomes meaningless. Robert was quickly approaching that stage. He was forgetting what day it was, only the window in his cell dictated day or night. Using the amount of light, he could predict accurately when the meals would show up. He was getting used to the meals and while it was nothing to brag about, he looked forward to what he called supper. Often it appeared to be leftovers from another meal, but most usually supper was the primary meal that provided leftovers for the next lunch. Nothing ever to brag about, but the meals were edible and he did get coffee regularly for breakfast and supper.

New Year's Day came and went. He heard some guns shot, saw the bon fires, and some revelers drinking and whooping it up. They were cautious not to get too close to the prison so as not to be mistaken for a break-out.

New Year's Day having reset Robert's internal clock, on what he determined to be the 3rd of January, two guards came to his cell and hustled him down the hall and to the same room where he and Hiram had visited. Sitting at the table in Hiram's chair was a surly looking one-armed Infantry Major. Robert couldn't help but think that must be the one-armed visitors' chair. The guards escorted Robert to his side of the table, and the guards snapped a salute to Major Inman, who responded briskly. He considered Robert's eyes and bellowed: "Report!"

It took Robert a minute to even understand what the Major was asking of him.

"Private Robert H. Edwards, Company E, First West Virginia Cavalry, Sir!"

"My name is Major Inman, I am assigned to the War Department, Washington DC as an investigator of internal affairs. I have been ordered to interrogate you and determine your status as a soldier and, more importantly, a loyal citizen of the United States of America."

Robert declared, “Sir, I am loyal to these United States of America.” He knew immediately based upon the look the Major threw back at him, that was not the appropriate time to be declaring his loyalty. He had yet to even begin to explain his circumstances.

“I, and I alone, will decide that, Private. I am going to put you under oath and you will be given the opportunity to explain your actions from July 2nd of the year 1863 until you were picked up on December 18th of the same year. I want the truth, the entire truth and nothing but the facts that are relevant to the situation. Is that understood?”

“Yes, Sir!”

After Robert had been given the oath and declared to tell the truth, nothing but the truth, so help him God, Major Inman instructed him to tell his story.

As Robert began, he went into more detail of the initial situation that ended up with him catching a ride to Towson town. He gave names and dates as best he could remember, and the Major wrote note after note. He would sometimes ask for minor clarifications but didn’t interrupt for great details until Robert had described the arrest on December 18th and incarceration in both Baltimore and here in Washington.

Feeling as if he had told everything important that had occurred in those six months, the first question Major Inman asked virtually floored Robert. He was almost speechless. He was indeed dizzy from surprise.

"Tell me about Miss Boyd!"

"Sir?"

"Did you not meet a Miss Belle Boyd while you were staying at Ady's Hotel? Did you not have a sexual encounter with same Belle Boyd and did you not share military information with said woman?"

"Whoa! How do you know anything about Miss Boyd? How did you know that I met her and that we might, and I am not saying that we did, have been intimate? How could you possibly know that?"

"Soldier, if nothing else, your reaction to the questions confirms what we might have speculated. However, speculation is not all that we have. On the day after your sexual encounter with Miss Boyd, we arrested her in the Ady's Hotel and brought her to this very prison. She was a guest of ours for a period and she was more than willing to tell us all about you and your sharing of information for sexual favors. We have you dead to rights, Private Edwards."

"Wait a minute, wait! I did not at any time trade

information for sex. We were both totally drained of fervor before we talked about anything to do with my background and what I knew. Specifically, I didn't have anything of consequence to tell her. I'm a Private who performed as a Teamster and then as a Clerk. I prepared letters and orders and other command letters for General Stahel, but the contents meant nothing to me. The orders were meaningless plus I couldn't have cared less. I liked my job as a Teamster much more, always on the go and accomplishing something that was appreciated by the men. I helped to keep them fed and their horses as well. Bottom line, I had nothing to tell her. But I don't understand why you would have arrested Belle in the first place."

"Private, we have it on solid evidence that Belle Boyd is a Southern spy and in fact, an officer in the Confederate Army. She admitted as much and told us that we could go straight to hell if we ever thought that she would take an oath to the United States of America. Here at Capitol Prison, we wanted to shoot her and be done with it. However, the War Department was having none of it and forced us to transport her back to Martinsburg, West Virginia, and at our expense. She obviously has a friend in high places that is protecting this young traitor. However, trust me, we are not done with her. She killed a soldier and thinks she got away with it. She was not punished but she will be or I will be damned. Belle Boyd has not heard the last of us nor of you. We will talk more later. Dismissed!"

While Robert was not an imbecile by any means, he could be as dismissive as any young man might be. He realized that this was not one of those times. This was a serious situation and perhaps even his life depended on it. He knew that he needed answers to their questions and that they had better be the answers they are looking for or he was in for a rough time.

He was amazed, even shocked, that Belle Boyd might be a spy. If she is, based on their shared experience, she should be very successful. Perhaps she should be a bit more selective in her subjects and she likely considered him "practice" but he certainly could live with that. He was up for more practice, help her hone her skills, per se. He didn't have anything to tell, so what could it hurt? Maybe he should think up some stuff, just so they would have something to talk about afterwards. Maybe he should straighten up before he ended up hanged for treason. Well, it was nice to fantasize.

23: Robert's First Train Ride

On the 17th of January 1864, a prison guard and two soldiers appeared at his cell door. The guard announced, "Grab your gear, Edwards, you are being transferred." Robert stood. Every piece of gear he owned in the world, he was wearing.

Robert traveled in handcuffs by train accompanied by the two soldiers, a corporal in charge and a mere private such as himself. He talked some with the corporal, who because of his position and responsibilities, didn't have much to share. Robert didn't know their destination and apparently the private, who was quite talkative, didn't either. Private Haynes was from Kansas and had joined the moment his folks agreed, and his father signed the papers. At 17, he was excited to be away from home and seeing the country. He liked his present duty assignment and figured that he had a decent chance of making it through the war intact if he could avoid getting into the infantry. Honestly, he had enlisted for the excitement, but the killing was not anything he was hoping to do. He shared his thoughts with Robert and it was one of several things they seemed to have in common.

When the conductor announced *Martinsburg, West Virginia*, Robert was told they were disembarking. Climbing down from the train, they were greeted by a lone private who was to take them the short distance to the jail.

Upon arrival, the soldiers and their prisoner were escorted to the Officer in Charge where the corporal presented his orders and turned over Private Robert H. Edwards. Under the scrutiny of his corporal, Private Haynes wished Robert good fortune and good bye. The escorts departed for their return trip to Washington. Robert was incarcerated without any fanfare.

Chapel bells were ringing in the distance when Robert was awakened. It wasn't quite daylight, but it wouldn't be long. It seemed safe to assume that it was Sunday morning in Martinsburg. Several days had passed since his arrival at the jail. If being basically ignored was the routine, it appeared that Robert had settled in.

There were other prisoners, but the jail was by no means overflowing with life of any kind. Overhearing others talking, Robert learned that the city had changed hands more than two dozen times thus far during the war. He wondered what happens to the prisoners when the opposing army takes control. Is everyone released, hanged, or retained regardless? Strange situation, for sure. It made Robert wonder, what were they thinking when they decided to transfer him here?

He was about to learn, and the reasoning would surprise him beyond words.

Monday morning after breakfast, Robert was escorted to what appears to be an interrogation room. One table and two chairs did little to fill the room. He noticed that the low hanging lamps were not directly over the table, which seemed to indicate that the room might have multiple uses. He is told to sit to one side of the table and is left alone in the room. After what he calculated to be ten minutes, footsteps approaching caught his attention and he moved forward in his chair. The door is opened quickly, and Major Inman walks briskly into the room, to the table as a guard orders

Robert to his feet.

The guard orders Robert to report! Major Inman quickly halts the process. "Never mind, soldier! Private Edwards and I are already acquainted. Isn't that correct, Edwards?"

Before Robert can muster a reply, Major Inman continues, "I told you in Washington that we were not done with you. Soldier, you may leave us alone. We have things to discuss and we will be a while."

The guard snaps a sharp salute, does an about face and departs the room briskly.

Major Inman's first question to Robert, "Have you been in touch with Belle Boyd?"

"Sir? I haven't been out of jail since I last talked with you. How would I have had any contact with anyone, let alone Belle? I requested and was denied pen and paper, so I couldn't even correspond with my family. I have been isolated."

"Would you have expected a deserter to have been treated any differently?"

"Major, I explained my situation and my actions to you in Washington. I was wounded and on the mend. I intended to return to my unit once I was healed and capable. I told you that I did not turn to the enemy and

I know that I can declare my allegiance to the USA and return to duty. I fully intended to do that!"

"Not so fast, Edwards. I told you that I and I alone would rule on your allegiance and we are a long way from that decision. I have more questions of you and your answers will certainly determine what the future holds for you. First, who is Hiram Robinett and what is your relationship to him?"

"Hiram? How do you know about Hiram?"

"Look, I know he visited you in Washington and he has been stirring things up through the 1st West Virginia Cavalry. What's the connection? Why is anyone paying attention to his queries?"

"Hiram and I were in Company E and we are from the same home town. We grew up together, enlisted together and worked together supporting our company. He was the Company E Commissary Sergeant and I was a regimental teamster. We kept our boys supplied and eating well. We were a good team until they made me a clerk.

"Hiram was promoted to Second Lieutenant, I transferred back from Brigade Headquarters and we were ordered to Gettysburg. Then all hell broke loose, we both were wounded. I became separated from my company and Hiram missed his promotion and was discharged. Supposedly he could no longer do his job. Ha! Hiram could do more work one handed than most men do with two. He's so smart that he could accomplish any task asked of him, and I suspect that is why people are listening to his questions."

"Why did he come to see you in Old Capitol and what did you tell him? What does he know about your situation and involvement with Miss Boyd?"

"Involvement? I am not involved with her! I met her in Baltimore as a part of my job and spent perhaps three hours of my life with her. I didn't know her before and I haven't seen or heard from her since, apart from what you allege of her, which I have no way of verifying. Thus far, she seemed much more trustworthy than you do, Sir!"

"Soldier, I understand that you are feeling a great deal of stress right now, but do not forget your military protocol. I am an officer in the United States Army and you will respond to me properly and with respect for my position, understand?"

"Sir, then don't accuse me of things that I did not do or of having relationships with someone who is not loyal to our country. She and I didn't discuss anything that led me to believe that she was anyone other than a young girl who was as attracted to me as I was her. That is all that it was, plain and simple."

"Well, Private Edwards, you got yourself into this mess and my superiors at the War Department are allowing me to give you an opportunity to get yourself out of it. Otherwise, you are an admitted deserter and we can, should we choose to do so, keep you incarcerated until hell freezes over. The choice just might be up to you."

Robert took time to think about what the Major was telling him, the situation and the idea of staying in this place forever. That certainly was not appealing.

"Okay, Major, what is it that you need from me?"

"This young traitor that you screwed is here in Martinsburg and we are about to arrest her again. We are going to find out exactly what her role is with the Rebs, her contacts here locally and within our forces. It is becoming apparent that someone of significance within our ranks has a special interest in Miss Boyd and we must find out who that is and what those interests are, other than the obvious. You are going to help us do that or your bacon will fry in your own grease. In the meantime, you will have no conversations with anyone other than me and no contacts with the outside world. Is that understood?"

"Well, obviously, you are in control of who can contact me and I don't know anyone here in Martinsburg."

"You know the most important person in your world and she is right here in Martinsburg. You will be seeing her soon! Keep your mouth shut until we talk again. You are dismissed!"

Once again, Robert is left wondering just how he ever got himself into this mess and how he was ever going to get out of it. Robert was certain that he should be worried. However, seeing as he had no way of controlling future events, he couldn't even figure out how he should react or what he should do. Therefore, Robert decided that he would worry about whether he had missed lunch. He had.

24: They Meet Again

The next morning, a Wednesday, Robert believed, there was a commotion down the corridor from his cell. He overheard other prisoners exclaiming "Woman in the house" and other less polite catcalls. Questioning a passing guard, Robert learned that they had brought a local woman in who is supposedly a southern sympathizer who might even be guilty of treason. Assured that she would not be housed in adjoining cell blocks, the guard assumed she was being escorted through more for effect than anything else. Scare her a bit.

Robert's immediate thought was that if this is indeed Belle Boyd, they wouldn't be scaring her anytime soon. Not from what he had seen of her.

Down at the end of the dark corridor, two guards escorted a beautiful young woman who continuously pushed their hands away as she walked a step ahead of them despite their best efforts to control her. As she approached and passed Robert's cell, he immediately recognized the beautiful Belle. However, regardless of what Robert might have hoped, Belle did not return any signs of recognition when passing. Robert didn't know what he was expecting but he was indeed disappointed. Then he found himself mad for expecting something from a girl who had just been arrested and was about to be thrown in jail again.

He also, defying all logic, found it extremely difficult to accept what they were saying about this innocent young girl.

Nothing else happened that day, other than the dull dreary weather both inside and out, skimpy meals and an occasional complaint from an inmate that would echo down the corridors.

Robert expected a visit from the Major but heard nothing for the next three days. Sunday morning brought chiming church bells and a stiff cold breeze across the prison court yard. Dried leaves blew around, but most were gone some time ago. A dog could be heard barking in the distance, but otherwise, the prisoners and the guards appeared to be alone with their thoughts of home, family, friends living and deceased. Thoughts of this "forever" war and what if anything was being accomplished that might bring it to a close.

Most things Robert was hearing indicated that Gettysburg and that horrible three days had defeated General Lee and the Southern Armies and that they were running from the inevitable surrender that had to be coming soon. He wondered what was to be gained by prolonging the death and destruction, all of which would have to be dealt with at some point. Why make it worse? It just didn't make sense to Robert to continue the pain and suffering to salvage pride. Damn the dignity. Stop the carnage. It seemed so simple. Obviously, it wasn't.

Robert was finishing up lunch, which was better than usual, even for a Sunday. A guard opened his cell door and proclaimed that he had a visitor. The guards never referred to Major Inman as a visitor, so Robert wasn't sure who this might be. Entering the familiar inter-rogation room, he was amazed, shocked to gaze upon Belle Boyd, the one and only.

Robert sat down on the opposite side of the table from Belle. The soldier who had been standing beside Belle explained the rules for the visit. "We have been instructed to leave the room so that you may talk privately. However, we will watch from the door and no touching is permitted and we will intervene if necessary. Do the two of you understand?"

Robert answered, "Yes" and Belle merely nodded her head. The soldier backed out of the room.

They sat quietly. Robert searched her face for any signs of recognition. If there was, Belle was doing an excellent job of disguising it.

Finally, when he could take it no longer, he asked, "Do you even remember me? Do you know who I am?"

"You're Robert, the deserter from Ady's Hotel. Of course, I know you."

"I should have told you then and I'll tell you now, I am not a deserter. I was injured and recovering from my wounds."

"Well, Robert, you are sure as hell in jail and that is what they do to deserters, isn't it?"

"Well, Belle, it appears to me that we are both in jail. I hear that you are far worse, a traitor, a spy and a southern sympathizer. I think you might be in more trouble than I am."

Finally, some life in those beautiful eyes. More like fire!

"How dare you! How dare you suggest that I am a traitor. I have been loyal to the great State of Virginia and the Confederate States of America from day one. I have not hidden, disguised and misled anyone as to where my loyalties lie. I am a Captain in the Confederate Army, appointed personally by General Jackson. I was awarded the Southern Cross of Honor. If anything, I am a prisoner of war and demand that I be treated as such and with the respect and considerations due an officer of the opposing forces. Ha! Traitor, indeed. And accused by a mere private, Please!"

"Wow, it's nice to have you talking and see some boil in your blood. Yep, I'm a Private and you knew that all along, so you can't make me feel lower than I am. I wasn't attempting to upset you. I am just telling you what people are saying and why I suspect you are here. What are they going to do to you? Has anyone told you anything?"

"They keep telling me that they know I have friends in the War Department and in the Union Forces that are protecting me and feeding me information to pass along to our Rebel Staff. They want to know who and how it is happening. If they think they can get information from me that is going to damage our chances for success, to win this war, they're nuttier than a fruit cake. That will never happen. They would have to hang me to shut me up and there are some who certainly would like to do that. Why did you ask to see me?"

"Belle, I didn't ask to see you. If you didn't ask to see me, then this was likely arranged by Major Inman. He is convinced that I have some special connection to you. He wants me to find out all those things you just talked about. For some reason, he thinks you will tell me all your deep dark secrets. He said you told him all about our encounter at Ady's. Why in God's name would you have done that? I didn't tell anyone because I thought things like that were special and not to be shared with others."

"Oh Robert, you inexperienced little man! What we did was fun, and I enjoyed it for what it was. An afternoon of fun with a young deserter. I had never been with a deserter before and the fact that you were a virgin as well was a bonus, for sure. But Robert, that is all that it was. Just a good time. I am sorry if you thought it was more. I really am."

For Robert, hearing this from Belle was hurtful and he felt foolish knowing that he would certainly still patch things up if he could. Ever the romantic, ever the dope.

"I don't know why I should be ashamed or embarrassed for being a virgin or inexperienced in the ways of the world. I was raised properly by my family and attended church and have never been in trouble with the law, until now, I guess." He wanted to add "which is apparently not the case with you" but he thought better of it.

"So, what are they going to do to you, Belle? Do you know? Have they said?"

"They are threatening to shoot me. I have some friends who are trying to interest the yanks in deporting me. I am helping them think that doing so (deporting me) would ruin my life, but if fact, if I can get to Europe, I might be able to help our cause. Another option is they are threatening to hang me by the neck. I'll tell you but never admit I said that I am scared that hanging might be their choice. I love my Virginia, but I am too young to die. If they deport me, I can easily live with that, and in fact, figure out how to use it to my advantage. Robert, if you tell anyone this, I have friends, even friends in here, who can and will hurt you."

"Belle, I'm not telling anyone anything that would put you in danger. I hoped you would figure that out by now. If you have something that you want me to pass along that will get them off both of our backs and maybe help us also, tell me what to say. Tell me what to do. I'll do it."

"Oh, Robert, another place, another time. I can see you are a good person plus I know you are good at bed repair. But, regardless, I have got to get out of this mess and if you can help yourself by helping me, fine. Just remember, if you help yourself by harming me, you will pay."

"Belle, you're hopeless but I guess I understand! Tell me what to do."

She laid out her plan.

25: Robert Plays Along

The following morning, before breakfast, Major Inman is back and questioning Robert for every detail of yesterday's meeting with Belle. Robert prayed that he could deliver Belle's plan in a manner that the major would believe.

"Captain Boyd is insisting that she be treated as a prisoner of war and be returned to her command as of the next scheduled exchange. She will never take the oath of allegiance and will be shot before ever supporting the USA again. She said that terms are non-negotiable, and she expects immediate action on her request."

Major Inman was visibly fuming. Robert expected snot to bubble from the Major's nose at any minute. Perhaps even smoke from his ears. Regaining his composure at least slightly, the Major took a deep breath, exhaled and spoke.

"The decision on Miss Boyd is out of my hands. They are going to deport her immediately, evidently to Canada. That decision doesn't make any sense to me whatsoever. Anyone can get across that border. It is open to all. What's to prevent her from returning and taking up her old habits. She is already responsible for a soldier's death. She should pay and I believe she should pay with her life."

"Major, what happens to me? I tried helping you but it was out of my hands. Can I get out of here and return to my unit? Can I repay my debt, fix my mistake by serving my country? I've learned my lesson and I am ready to do my duty as I originally signed up for and would have been doing except for a dropped grenade."

"Edwards, Washington has prevented me from doing my duty. They know Boyd is guilty of treason, is a spy, has killed a U.S. soldier, and is our enemy. I can't do anything about her, but I sure as hell can do something about you. They won't let me hang you or shoot you, but you sure as shit can stay in this prison until the end of the war. I'm done with you. Dismissed."

"Well, Crap!" Confusion raced through Robert's

mind. He didn't know for sure just how he should feel. In his opinion, Belle was elevated in his mind. How did she do it. Who helped her? How does she have this much influence in the government in Washington? This is exactly what she had told Robert was going to happen. She missed on destinations. She figured England, it turned out to be Canada. Not bad!

So, apparently ends the saga of "La Belle Rebelle", or at least in the life of Robert H. Edwards. Additionally, if Major Inman is to be believed, is the possibility of freedom. He wasn't extremely upset with the likelihood of sitting in jail in Martinsburg until the end of the war. The war couldn't last forever, could it?

Small issues, such as what if the Rebs win, could present a problem but he was certain that he could talk his way out of the situation if necessary. After all, he was a deserter, wasn't he?

An artillery captain, injured at the first battle of Bull Run, oversaw the prisoners incarcerated in the Martinsburg Court House facility. Captain Heidel called Private Edwards to his office on the 1st day of March.

"Private, I understand that you served as clerk for General Stahel."

"Yes, Sir, I did."

"I need assistance here. My current clerk has been released and my staff is depleted. I want you to fill in and if things go well, you can have the position. There are obvious advantages to helping. Certain benefits are made available for good performance and earned trust can pay off as well. I could order you to take the position but having someone who wants the opportunity makes it much easier on everyone. How about it!"

"Sir, my father was the Postmaster in my hometown and he received recognition and rewards for years because of the job he done. He advised me to never let a good opportunity pass you by without giving it a try. Yes, Sir, I would love to have the job."

"Good. The desk in the outer office is yours. I made a list of tasks, first the daily, then the weekly, followed by the monthly. There are of course unexpected special demands that must be answered promptly and correctly, but we'll get through those and you will be expected to catch on quickly. Still interested?"

"Yes, Sir!"

"Then, let's get to it!"

That is how Robert H. Edwards became the clerk for the Military Commander in charge of the Martinsburg Court House Jail. Captain Heidel was a good boss, he was fair and reasonable and wasn't at all opposed to jumping in and helping when it was needed, such as on a short fuse item.

Robert, who was used to the urgency of the headquarters staff of General Stahel, took to this far less stressful job quite easily. Within 30 days, certainly 60 days, he had the requirements down to a pattern and was finding himself with a fair amount of spare time. Captain Heidel had let him deliver reports and other items throughout the court house and on a fine mid-April morning allowed Robert to leave the courthouse building for the first time since his incarceration. Given the rest of the morning and a city map, Robert headed down King Street to see what the city had to offer.

The war had not been kind to Martinsburg. Having changed hands near three dozen times had taken a toll on the homes and businesses in the area. While not a ghost town, there had obviously been far more people here before the fighting started.

The Baltimore and Ohio Train Depot complex had been destroyed. The tracks had only recently been replaced and a temporary depot served the area.

Robert enjoyed his excursion and new-found freedom. Seeing normal people living their lives as normally as possible was comforting and Robert decided he might re-visit Martinsburg one day once the war was over and things returned to normal.

The Invalid Corps, which was the forerunner of the VRC (Veteran Reserve Corps), was organized under authority of General Order No. 105, War Department, dated April 28, 1863. It was designed to utilize former soldiers who could no longer perform all the duties required but could be of service performing administrative-type functions.

22nd Regiment Veterans Reserve Corps
Organized at Washington, D.C., January 12, 1864

When Hiram arrived back in Washington, he had good news waiting. He had been accepted to join the 22nd VRC and would be returning to active duty on March 9, 1864, just two and a half months after turning 21 years old. There was no position open for a 1st Lieutenant but he would retain his current rank, which was pleasing to hear. He looked forward to getting back into the war effort, and doing what he could to make a difference or at least contribute.

VRC Orders

War Department
Provost Marshal General's Office
Washington, D.C. March 14, 1864

2nd Lieut Hiram Robinette.
Invalid Corps having reported for duty
In obedience of orders the Provost Marshal
General directs that he will proceed to
Cliffburne Barracks Washington DC there
report to Col. George C. Woodward,
Commanding - for duty

M.R. Wisewell
Colonel and Assistant to
Provost Marshal General

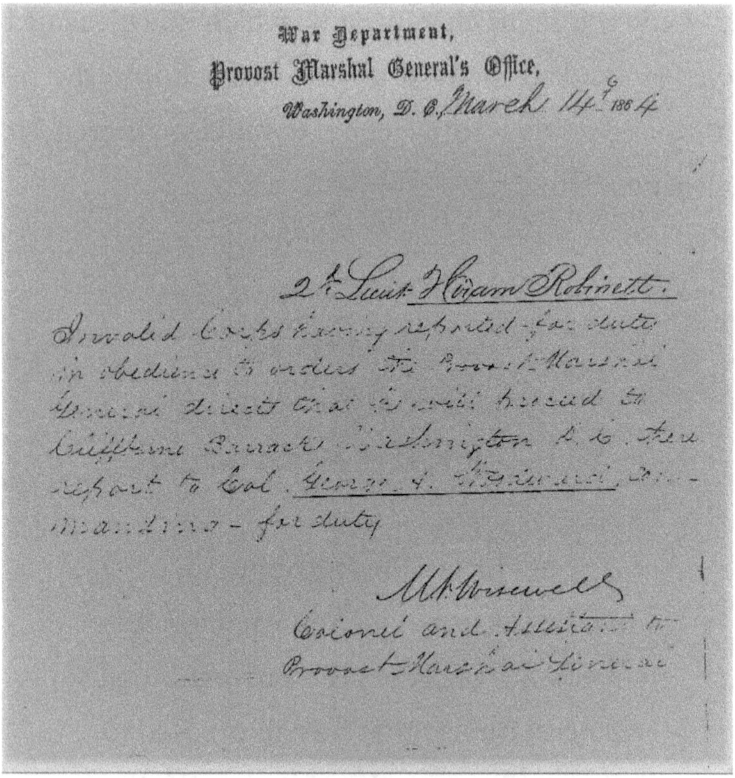

War Department,
Provost Marshal General's Office,
Washington, D. C., March 14th 1864

2d Lieut. Hiram Robinett.
Invalid Corps having reported for duty
in obedience to orders the Provost Marshal
General directs that you will proceed to
Cliffburne Barracks Washington D. C. there
report to Col. George [illegible] [illegible] commanding — for duty

M. N. Wisewell
Colonel and Assistant to
Provost Marshal General

VRC Orders. Source: www.archives.com

Hiram was immediately given command of a detail responsible for ensuring that the Aqueduct Bridge was secure and anyone entering the city possessed proper authority to do so.

Aqueduct Bridge 1864. Source: Library of Congress

Aqueduct Bridge 1864. Source: Library of Congress

Report to Provost Marshal – May

Head Quarters Guard Aqueduct Bridge
Georgetown, DC May 24, 1864
Col T. Jugraham, Provost Marshal

Colonel,

I send under guard Citizen M Donelson. He was arrested by the guard at the bridge for trying to pass without a pass or the countersign. He claims to be a wagon master and has in his position a good horse which I send to you. Said Donelson was intoxicated at the time of his arrest.

I have the honor to be
Your obt Servant
Hiram Robinett
Lieutenant Commanding Guard
Aqueduct Bridge

Note: Citizen Donelson was reprimanded and released.

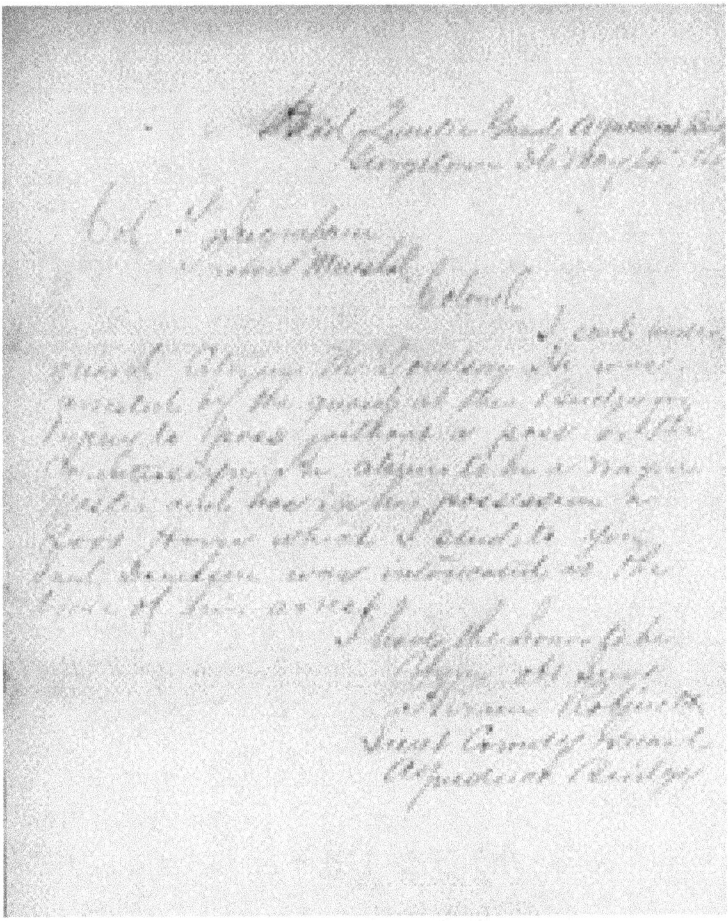
Colonel

Report to Provost Marshal - May 1864.

Source: www.archives.org

Report to Provost Marshal - July

Head Quarter Guard Aqueduct Bridge
Georgetown, DC July 2, 1864
Col T Jugraham
Provost Marshal

Colonel

I have the honor to forward you under guard Citizen George Butterfield who appears at this bridge without a pass or the countersign.

I have the honor to be
Very Respectfully
Your obedient Servant
Hiram Robinett
Lieutenant Commanding Guard
Aqueduct Bridge

Note: George Butterfield was arrested and prosecuted for illegally entering the city

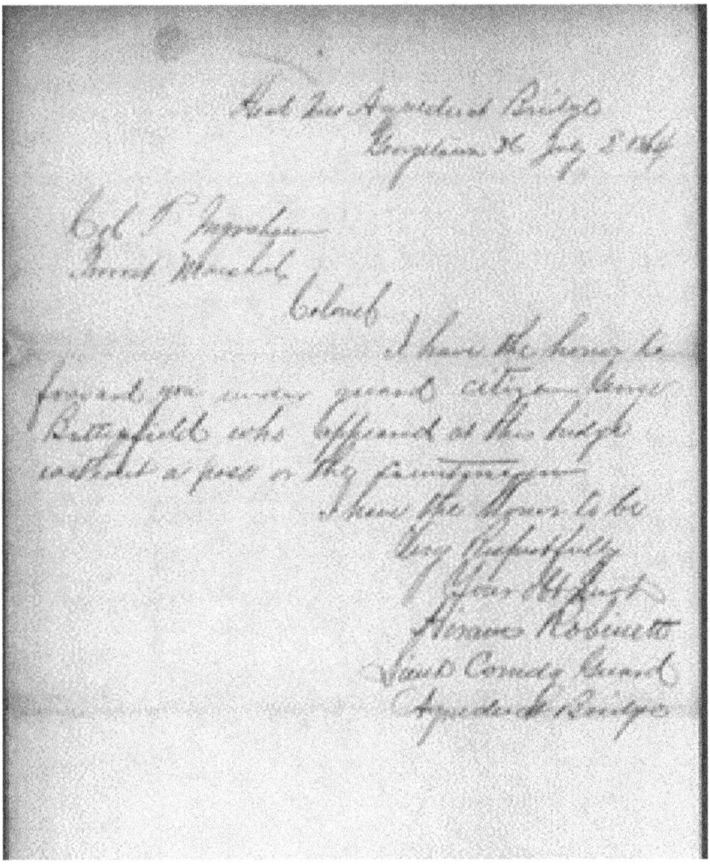

Head Qrs Aqueduct Bridge
Georgetown DC July 8 1864

Col T Ingraham
Provost Marshal

Colonel

I have the honor to forward you seven [illegible] citizens from Battlefield who appeared at the bridge without a pass or [illegible]

I have the honor to be
Very Respectfully
Your Obt Servt
Horace Robinett
Lieut County Guard
Aqueduct Bridge

Report to Provost Marshal - July 1864.

Source: www.archives.gov

Hiram received the official notification of his commission and signed receipt of his Commission to 2nd LT, 22nd VRC signed by Abraham Lincoln and Secretary of War Stanton.

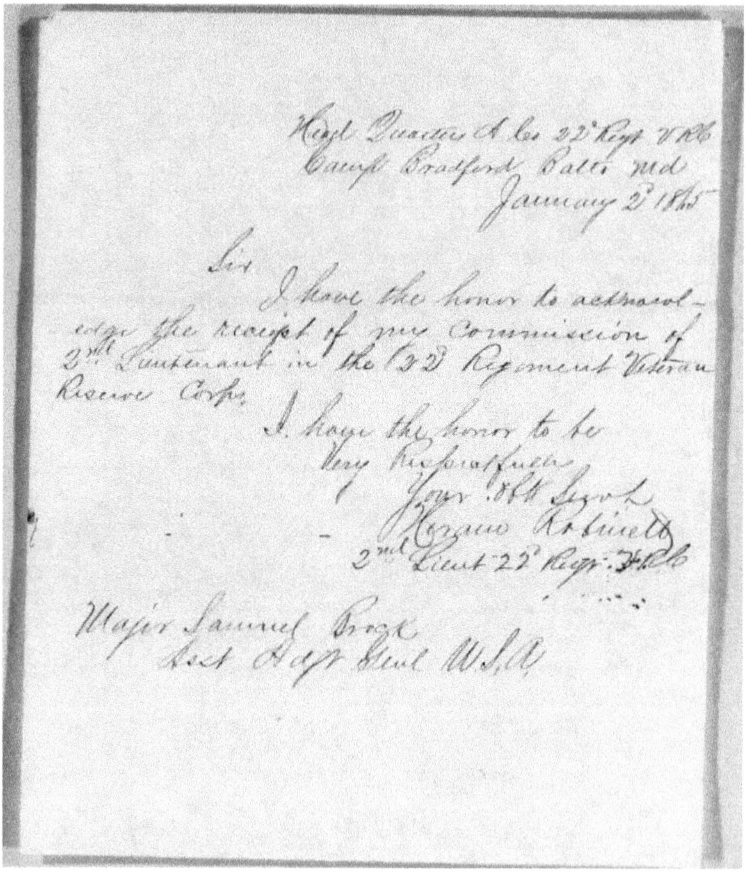
Head Quarters A Co 22d Regt VRC
Camp Bradford Balto Md
January 2d 1865

Sir
I have the honor to acknowledge the receipt of my Commission of 2nd Lieutenant in the (22) Regiment Veteran Reserve Corps.
I have the honor to be
Very Respectfully
Your Obt Servt
Hiram Robinette
2nd Lieut 22d Regt VRC

Major Samuel Breck
Asst Adjt Genl U.S.A.

Official Commission Receipt. Source: www.archives.gov

This would have been the second such document that Hiram received, the first being when he was commissioned with the 1st Virginia Volunteer Cavalry in January 1863. The location of the first document remains a mystery.

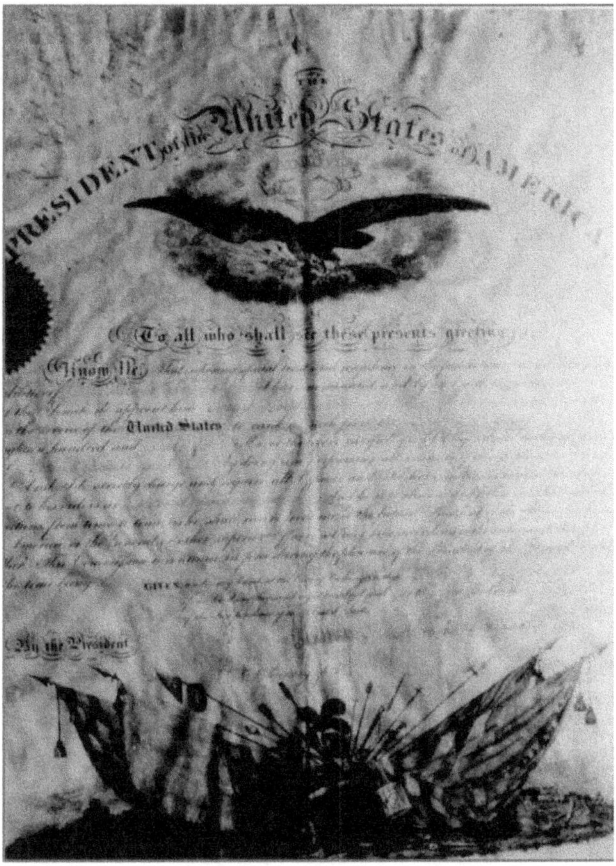

Commission Document. Property of Sandra Lake.

In late July 1864, Hiram was given the opportunity to assume command of Company A which was stationed in Baltimore, Md. He applied and provided Lt. Col. Rutherford with his military experience. It was significant enough to get him the job and he was assigned the position and responsibility on November 8, 1864.

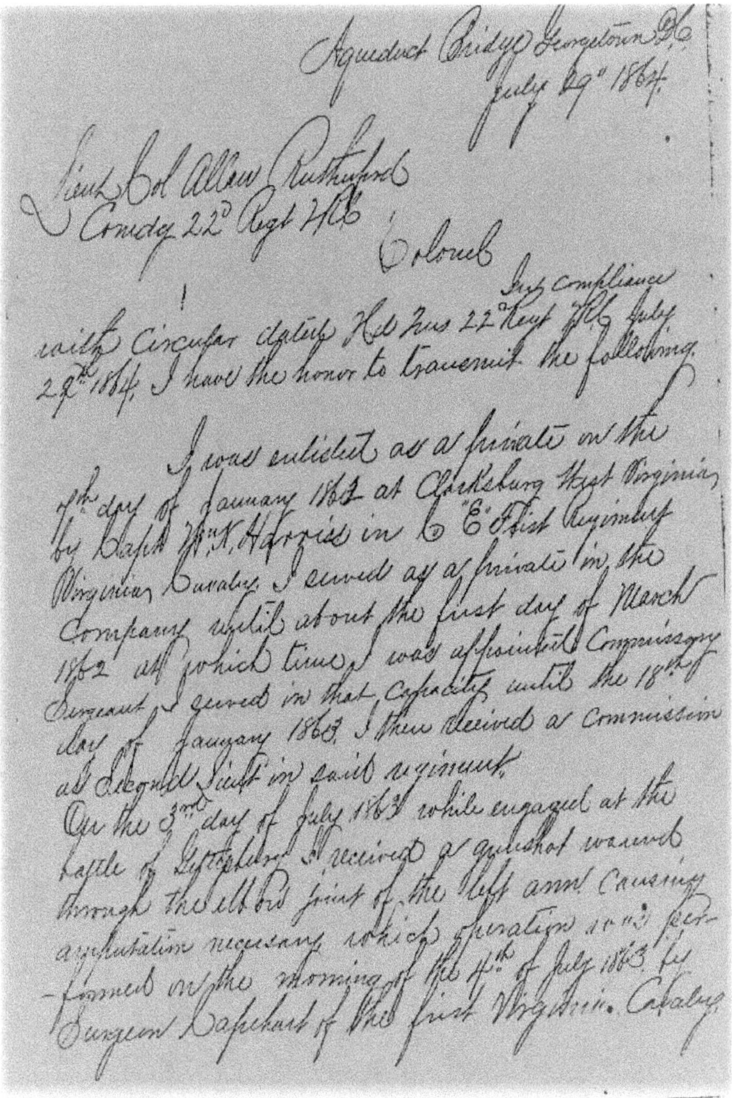
Aqueduct Bridge Georgetown D.C.
July 29th 1864.

Lieut Col Allen Rutherford
Comdg 22d Regt V.R.C.

Colonel

In compliance with Circular dated Hd Qrs 22d Regt V.R.C. July 29th 1864. I have the honor to transmit the following.

I was enlisted as a private on the 7th day of January 1862 at Clarksburg West Virginia by Capt Wm. N. Harris in Co "E" First Regiment Virginia Cavalry. I served as a private in the Company until about the first day of March 1862 at which time I was appointed Commissary Sergeant. I served in that capacity until the 18th day of January 1863. I then received a Commission as Second Lieut in said regiment.

On the 3rd day of July 1863 while engaged at the battle of Gettysburg I received a gunshot wound through the elbow joint of the left arm causing amputation necessary which operation was performed on the morning of the 4th of July 1863 by Surgeon Capehart of the first Virginia Cavalry.

Military experience. Source: www.archives.gov

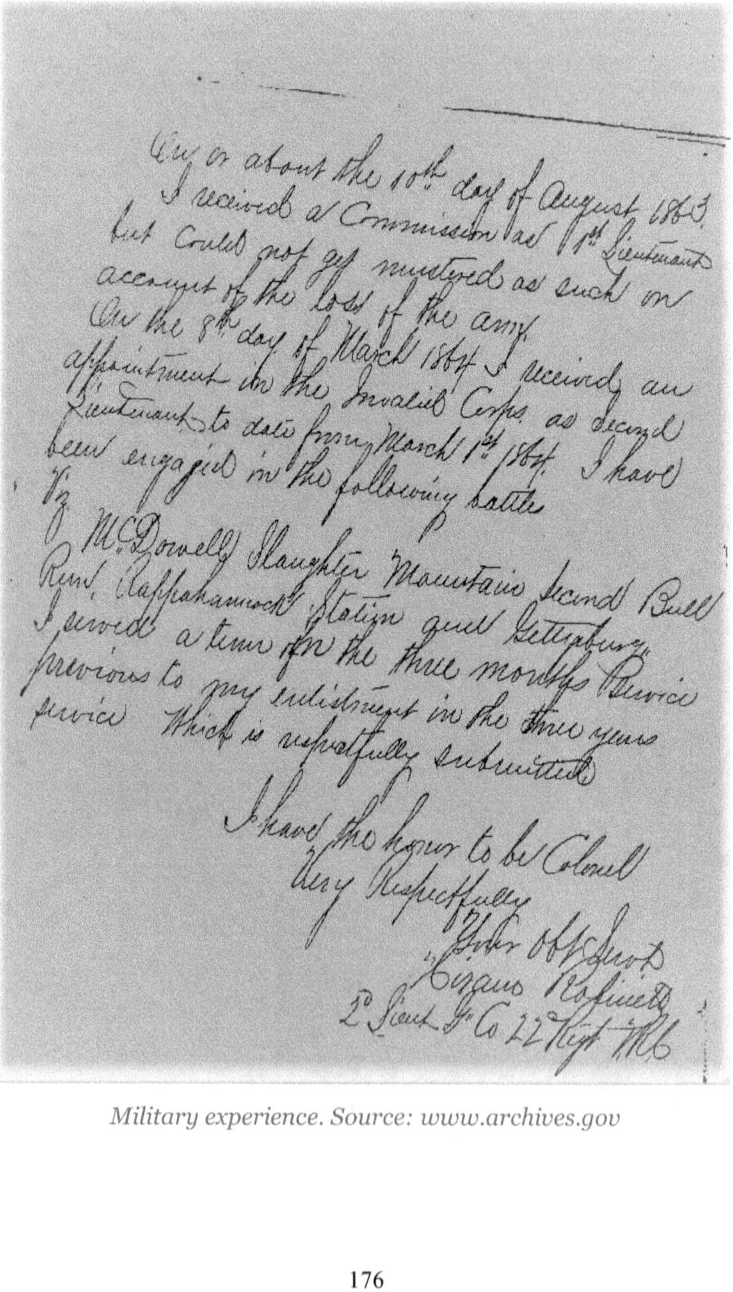

On or about the 10th day of August 1863
I received a Commission as 1st Lieutenant
but Could not get mustered as such on
account of the loss of the army.
On the 8th day of March 1864 I received an
appointment in the Invalid Corps as second
Lieutenant to date from March 1st 1864. I have
been engaged in the following battle
Viz
McDowell, Slaughter Mountain, Second Bull
Run, Rappahannock Station and Gettysburg.
I served a term for the three months service
previous to my enlistment in the three years
service Which is respectfully submitted

I have the honor to be Colonel
Very Respectfully
Your Obt Servt
Lorenzo Robinett
2d Lieut I Co 22 Regt [illegible]

Military experience. Source: www.archives.gov

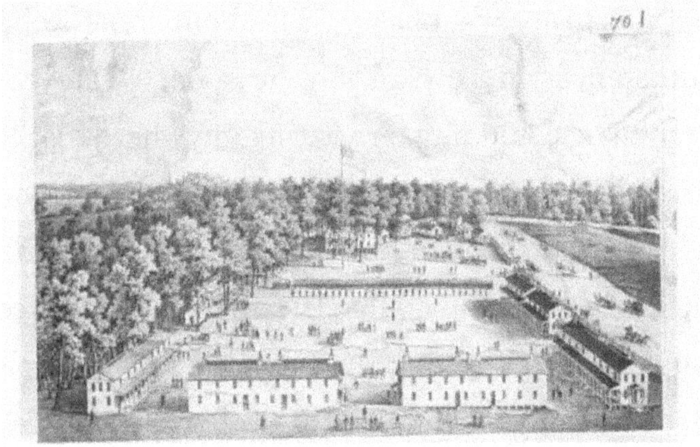

Camp Bradford, Baltimore. Source: www.archives.gov

Company A, 22nd VRC was located at Camp Bradford in Baltimore, Maryland. The company was responsible for traveling to locations from the extreme Northeast to the Midwest to pick up and transport recruits to rendezvous points in the field. It was a continuous effort to deliver fresh troops to the Army as quickly and as safely as possible. It required good communications skills, long hours in the saddle, knowledge of the areas and an ability to avoid the enemy at all costs. It was not an easy job and came with a significant amount of related stress.

Hiram was used to stress and performing under

extreme conditions to accomplish his goals. One task that he decided to tackle before he was offered command was to see what he could find out about Robert's circumstances in Towson. So, he spent whatever leisure time he could muster visiting anywhere that Robert mentioned he had been. He tried tracking down the folks who had helped care for Robert and gathered what information he could. Hiram knew that a court martial would be coming and he wanted to be prepared if there was anything he might do to help his lifelong friend.

27: LT ROBINETT DEFENDS PVT EDWARDS

Sure enough, in late September 1864, in Martinsburg, Western Virginia, Lt. Hiram Robinett was given the opportunity to represent Private Robert H. Edwards in a Court Martial Proceeding. Charged with desertion on July 2, 1863, at Gettysburg, Pennsylvania, Robert faced a dishonorable discharge, loss of an Army pension, and perhaps worse.

"Colonel, Major, members of the convening court martial of Private Robert H. Edwards. I am 2nd Lieutenant Hiram Robinett, of Company G, 22nd Veteran Reserve Corps. I am here to testify on behalf of Private Edwards concerning the charges of desertion on July 2, 1863.

Court martial board. Source: www.archives.gov

"Company records of Company E, 1st West Virginia Volunteer Cavalry, of which we both served, clearly indicate that on the morning of July 2nd, Private Edwards was one of an eight-man squad assigned picket duty approximately two miles northeast of the town of Gettysburg. He accompanied Corporal Dropsy on a patrol of the picket line. Approximately one mile out, they encountered and were attacked by a group of Rebels. Corporal Dropsy was killed and Edwards was hit by artillery of some nature, likely a grenade.

"Edwards was rendered unconscious and when he awakened, he was suffering from concussion and unable to make a conscience decision as to what to do, not knowing if he was in friendly or enemy territory. He apparently again lost consciousness and was found by a family, placed on their wagon and eventually taken to Towson town, Maryland.

"In Baltimore, I was able to locate Mr. Wilburn Booth who verified this story in total. I spoke with Mr. Booth's daughter, Melinda, who described the serious nature of the injury, the fact that Private Edwards was delirious, unable to comprehend and maintain logic of any kind, and was a very sick man. The leg was treated and has healed but will never be totally well. Private Edwards walks with a pronounced limp and continues to suffer frequent pain.

"The Booths left Private Edwards at the Ady's Hotel in Towson town. I interviewed the Hotel Manager who verified Robert's employment and loyalty. When Miss Booth returned in December, she was informed that Private Edwards had been arrested by the Army and taken away. She knew not where or how to contact him. She visited the Baltimore jail and tried to tell her story, explaining the circumstances, but there was no interest as Edwards was no longer there.

"Gentlemen, I have known Robert Edwards my entire life, minus the year I am older than he. We are from the same home town and grew up together. We attended school together, hunted and fished together and are good friends. We went to Parkersburg and enlisted in the 1st West Virginia Cavalry, Company E together. I tell you all of this to ensure you that I know what I am talking about when I speak of Robert Edwards.

"Robert is not a coward. He is not a deserter. He was selected to clerk for General Stahel at brigade headquarters. General Stahel could have picked any number of soldiers. He selected Edwards because of his performance, his loyalty, his reputation and the fact that he was a good soldier.

"It is important that you know this man before deciding his fate. He admitted to desertion for the simple fact that his character demanded that he admit that he had let his company, his fellow-soldiers, and his country down. The guilt that he felt is not because he made a cowardly decision to desert. The guilt felt was because he was unable to hurry back, which he intended to do but was unable to accomplish because of his injury.

"Note that had Robert returned earlier, he would

have been discharged because of his inability to perform his duties. I relate personally as I was discharged because of injuries received at Gettysburg. I felt that same guilt until I was permitted to come back on active duty with the VRC.

"In summation, Robert Edwards is a good man, a loyal citizen who is willing and ready to take the oath of allegiance, and get back to doing his part to save our great union. That's all that I have. Thank you."

Within two hours, the board came back with the only reasonable decision available to them. The official record reads as follows:

Robert H. Edwards, Pvt, 1st West Virginia Cavalry, Company E has been honorably acquitted by a general Court Martial of the Charges preferred against him. Robert H. Edwards, Co E 1 W Va. Cav is hereby released from arrest and returned to duty without loss of pay or emoluments.

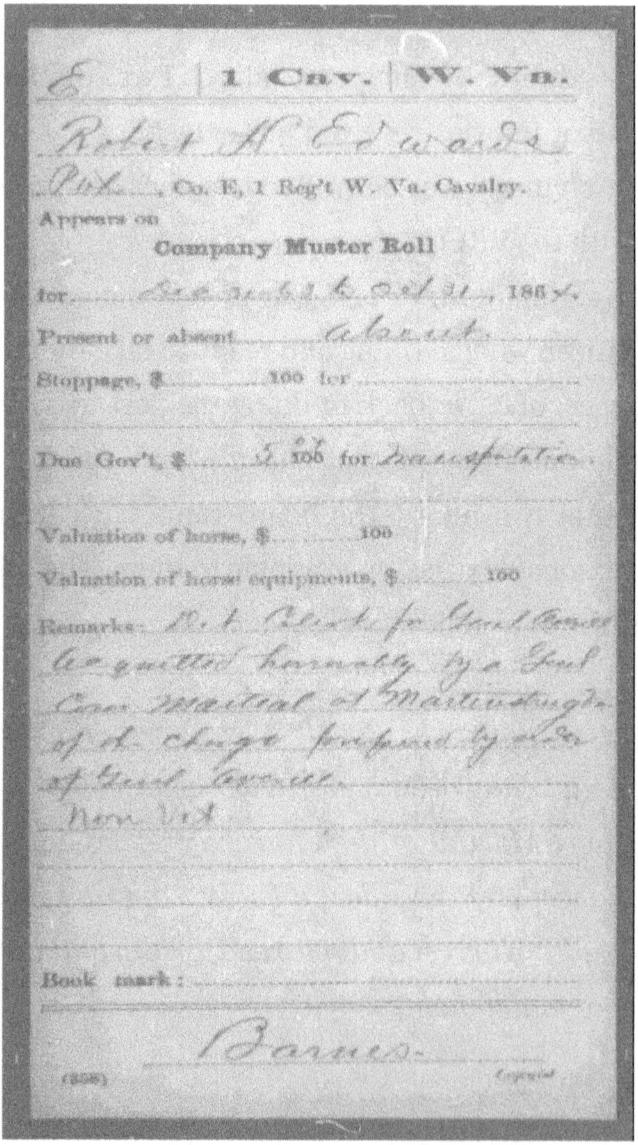

E | 1 Cav. | W. Va.

Robert H. Edwards

Pvt., Co. E, 1 Reg't W. Va. Cavalry.

Appears on

Company Muster Roll

for Dec 31 63 to Oct 31, 1864.

Present or absent absent

Stoppage, $ ...... 100 for

Due Gov't, $ 5 07/100 for transportation.

Valuation of horse, $ 100

Valuation of horse equipments, $ 100

Remarks: Rel. Clerk for Genl Conner Acquitted honorably by a Genl Court Martial at Martinsburg of the charge preferred by order of Genl Averell.

Non Vet

Book mark:

Barnes
Copyist

(358)

Source: www.archives.gov

28: Surprise of a Lifetime

Tears trickled down Robert's face although he attempted to maintain his composure. The past year and three months had been tough on him, perhaps even harder than he realized. He shook hands with Hiram and then let his emotions get the best of him and he hugged his best friend, the man who had certainly and once again came through for him.

Hiram grabs Robert by the shoulders and gives him a gentle but firm shake. "Hey, buddy, you need to get yourself together. There is someone outside that wants to see you."

"Who wants to see me? I only know one other person in this town and I don't even think she is here anymore. They shipped her to Canada."

"No. This person came with me from Baltimore.

More accurately, this person came from Towson town."

As they walked together into the court house hallway, a beautiful tall slender blonde turned to face them. Instant recognition flashed in her eyes and she hurried to close the distance between them. Bright blue eyes flashed as Melinda Booth dazzled them with a gorgeous smile.

"Well, I take it that your friend is no longer a deserter. I don't see shackles or cuffs."

Hiram replied with as close to humor as he could muster, "No, I convinced him to plead insanity and they bought it. He is a free man, back in the Army but a free man."

Something very rare for Robert occurred. He was speechless. He stood in awe, looking between his very best friend and the most beautiful woman he had ever seen and one that he never expected to see again.

Recovering somewhat but still giddy to say the least, Robert mumbled. "Melinda. Mindy. What are you doing here? How did Hiram find you? What are you doing here? Gosh lady, you are so beautiful! What are you doing here?"

"You really do need to expand your vocabulary. You keep repeating yourself, but I did like the *beautiful* comment. That was good. Lt. Robinett came and found us, north of Baltimore. He talked with my father and with me and I guess we convinced him that you were not a deserter but an injured soldier. When he told me that General Averill had scheduled your court martial and that there was a chance you might hang, I thought I might come along and finally see you dance."

"Ha! I can see that you haven't lost your sense of humor these past months. Wow, I can't believe that you are here. I am so happy to see you. I have not forgotten how well you cared for me and then dumped me like a hot potato. Can I give you a hug?"

"You had better. I didn't ride all this way with Hiram to shake your hand. I have thought about you often and even came to see you twice, but you were not there and then they said you were arrested. I didn't think this day would ever happen. Hug me!"

Hug her he did. At first it was somewhat reservedly, but that changed quickly. Robert had forgotten what it was like to hug a female. Hiram was the last person he had hugged, and that was very forgettable. No offense but he was fairly certain that Hiram was just not into hugging.

Mindy felt warm and she smelled heavenly. He

started to pull away and felt her tighten her hold. Robert's head was spinning. "I have to tell you something Mindy. I am right now totally confused. So much has happened and it seems like my entire life has been waiting for this minute. You look so wonderful, words can't explain it. I mean, you know you are beautiful. Why are you here? Why are you here to see me?"

"Robert! I guess if we are going to talk this seriously, we should stop hugging. I can't explain how strange this is, how strange it has been for me as well. Since meeting you, since caring for you, I cannot seem to get you out of my mind. I have been helping at the hospitals, treating other soldiers and so many of them are in terrible agony, both mentally and physically. It is terrible what this war is doing to so many young innocent boys who will never be young or innocent again. But as I found myself helping these young men, I always kept going back to when I took care of you. I think I realized at some point that I wasn't thinking about helping you, I was thinking about you, Robert Edwards. I couldn't get you out of my mind and I'm thinking that maybe I can't get you out of my heart. So, I thought, when Hiram gave me the chance, that I should come see you and let you know. It is silly, I know, but not nearly as silly as thinking about you and never letting you know. What would that accomplish other than me becoming an old spinster. So, anyway, Robert, here I am. Say something, say anything!"

"Melinda, the first time I opened my eyes and looked into yours, I realized that I was looking at the most beautiful creature in the world. The entire world. Since I last saw, you have matured into a lovely woman. Someone like me, a lowly Private, I couldn't ever do enough, accomplish enough, grow enough to deserve someone of your beauty, your intelligence, your personality. I would never be worthy of your love, never live up to your expectations. I have plans but they are not big enough, bold enough to deserve you. How could I ever earn your respect, let alone your love."

"Well, you can certainly begin by giving yourself a little credit. You got through this thing without a scratch, given a bad knee or so. Hiram said that you will receive all your back pay, so you're on your way to having a little nest egg. You can start making plans for when this vicious war ends. Life will go on.

"What say we try this, if you are at all interested in me. Hiram must leave for Baltimore tomorrow on the train. I am scheduled to go as well, but I could change my ticket and stay a day or so. If you could get some time off, we could spend some time together and see if we might be compatible. We could both see if we want to pursue whatever this is, I mean if we even like each other. What do you think?"

"Actually, I was thinking that I might start taking dance lessons."

"You remembered!"

"Melinda, I remember most everything. One of my traits. I remember your breathing, the number of your steps from the door to the bed, your curls laying on your shoulders, the blue in your eyes. Believe me, I remember. Your laughter, your smell, I remember!"

"Okay. Okay. I believe you", Mindy giggled. "So, does this mean you agree to my plan? Will you show me around Martinsburg?"

"Ma'am, I would love to! Where will you stay? We'll have to find you a room."

"I already have a room. Hiram and I arrived last night. I told the desk clerk that I would likely be staying another night or two. It pays to be prepared plus I was fairly certain you wouldn't pass up a great deal! And believe me, young man, I am a great deal!"

"Mindy, no man in the entire universe would doubt

that for a minute. I'll have to check with Captain Heidel and see if I can get a few days off to celebrate my new-found freedom. Don't worry, if he says 'No', I'll desert."

"Robert, that is not funny!" But it was. It really was and they all laughed. Even Hiram.

Hiram stated that he had an errand to run and that he would meet up with them for dinner. His treat.

Robert, recently having been a prisoner, had not a penny to his name. His only available option was eating at the court house jail, so he decided he could wait if need be. He certainly wanted to stay with Mindy for as long and as close as he possibly could. Robert was having a very hard time accepting what had transpired thus far this day, and as happy as he was, he was quickly wearing out.

They agreed on a place to eat directly across the street from the court house and Hiram was off. Mindy, sensing Robert's dismay, suggested they walk and talk.

29: Walking and Talking

"How about that tour you promised me." She grabbed his arm and moved close to him, kissing him lightly on the cheek. As tired as he had been, it was gone. He had never felt such energy as the adrenaline surged through his body. He was embarrassed as to where all that energy seemed to be headed and he hoped that Mindy didn't notice. They walked.

They walked up King Street, taking in the sights including the destruction from the war. They talked. Robert asked about her father and her young brother. Her father was fine but feeling the effort involved with uprooting his family and beginning over at an age where he should be preparing to be an elderly land baron instead of an old farmer. Her young brother was all excited about the war and wanted to join as a musician. So far, father had refused to sign and it didn't seem likely anytime soon.

Robert talked about news from his folks and things in Chauncey, Ohio. Mindy commented that she would like to visit there one day and again, Robert's head began to spin. Could she really be serious about this, about them and about the future? What did he possibly do to deserve even a look from her, let alone the possibility of spending his life with her? This is nuts. This is crazy. He was thinking that if he ever had a doubt, those doubts no longer existed. There is a God. There must be because what else could explain this miracle that was happening to him this very day, September 27, 1864.

Suddenly they were kissing. On King Street, in front of the court house, in front of God and everybody. It started slow, gently, and rapidly grew in fervor. Neither Robert or Melinda expected this, planned this, it just erupted. It was intense. It was natural. It was spontaneous and it was wonderful. As she nipped his lower lip, the shock of pain brought him somewhat to his senses. He gently pushed her to arm's length, looking deeply into those pretty blue eyes which appeared to be on fire.

He asked, “Are you really hungry?”

She laughed that amazing laugh and replied softly, “No, not in the least!”

Another deeper voice interrupted. “Well, you better be, because I am!” Hiram had appeared, seemingly out of nowhere, but actually out of the court house.

“I talked with Captain Heidel and got you two days off. Check in each day before noon and report back to work on Friday. Now let’s go eat before the two of you are thrown in jail for indecent exposure. Christ, and in front of the court house jail. I swear!”

Again, everyone laughed as they crossed the dirt street and walked into the restaurant.

For Robert, it seemed like the longest dinner he had ever eaten. Mindy seemed fine and in no hurry for the evening to end. Hiram appeared to be taking his time and enjoying making Robert squirm in his chair.

Hiram asked, “So, Robert, what do you have planned for the rest of the evening?”

Before he can answer, Mindy offers, “He will likely go back to the jail, have a restless, sleepless night, and come see you off in the morning.”

Robert dejectedly replies, “Yep, I guess so. What time does your train leave?”

Melinda laughs heartily, "Not on your life, Robert. I found you and you are staying in my sight until I must go home. I may be a brazen hussy, but you are staying with me."

This caused Hiram to laugh, a deep throaty laugh that caught all three of them by surprise.

Hiram regains his almost constant composure. "We had better get out of here before they are forced to throw us out!"

Mindy and Robert laughed, she gathers her things and they slowly walk back to their hotel. Robert would have preferred to run but figured that might be a little too obvious.

It was a beautiful full moon as they walked King Street back to the Hotel. Reaching the steps to the large front porch, Hiram said his goodbyes.

Robert began, "Hiram, you saved my life today. Without you, I could have rotted in jail until this endless war is finally over. I would likely have been kicked out. You always seem to end up taking care of me. Maybe one day, I'll actually grow up and at least be a shadow of the man that you are."

"Robert, I am glad that I could help set the record straight. I owed you that much. I kind of lost my way and disowned you for a bit while you were missing. I began to believe what the Army was saying. I knew better and I finally came to my senses and did something about it. I should have done it long before now."

"Hiram, I owe you so much and now, I owe you for bringing Melinda to me and now I even owe you for dinner. Thank you so much and I will repay you, one day, somehow."

Mindy interjects, "Are you two going to kiss or what?"

That succeeded in breaking the mood, and once again, the three friends laughed.

Hiram finally broke away, yelling back at them before he disappeared into the hotel. "Melinda, it has been wonderful meeting you. Take care of my buddy! Robert, tell the Wheelers hello from me. Night!"

30: The Whole Story

Mindy suggested they sit for a while. They picked a swing at the end of the long veranda, away from the other guests.

"Robert, I have some things to tell you that will explain a few things for you. I am not a woman of the world. The girl that you have seen and hopefully enjoyed being with today is not really who I am. There is not a long list of pursuers that you need to beat to win my heart. I am near certain that you already have it.

"When I was 13 years old, just a young girl and very naïve and trusting, an older neighbor boy raped me. I told my father and he literally went into a rage, tracked the boy down and beat him to death. The judge ruled it justified but it changed my dad and it changed me. I had no desire for something like that to ever happen to me again."

"Melinda, you don't have to tell me all of this. I like you just the way you are. You are the most beautiful thing that has ever happened to me and I want to be with you. I will take care of you."

"Robert, I need to tell you this. Hush, and listen. That incident was very traumatic for me. It would be for any child. I had no desires whatsoever, from that time until I laid eyes on you in our wagon and helped Dad carry you into the hotel.

"I sat next to your bed and hopefully helped nurse you back to health. I spent long hours with you and I felt myself developing feelings for you, for your hair, your lips, your chest and arms. I saw all of you while you were sleeping. I initially thought that those feelings were because I was helping you get well. I realized finally that it was more than that. I realized that I wanted you. I wanted you healthy. I wanted you awake and holding me. I had held you in your sleep and I wanted you to hold me as well. I wanted you to give me back what that boy took away, the ability to love, to be sexually excited and to be sexually active. I wanted you to be my first and hopefully my only lover."

Robert tried to speak.

"Hush, I'm almost done. Robert, when you came into my life, I thought that I was healing you. I finally realized that you were healing me. I came here to continue my therapy and perhaps in the mean-time, convince you that you want to spend the rest of your life with me, as I do with you."

"Melinda, is it okay if I call you Melinda. Mindy just seems too casual for me. Melinda shows off the class and beauty that you have. I want you to know that you are more than just Mindy to me.

I'm going to tell you something that I hope doesn't hurt you because that is not the point in telling you. I want to be completely honest and that takes getting this off my chest."

"Fine, tell me!"

"When you found me in the back of your wagon, I was a virgin. I had never been with anyone. I chased a sheep one time but couldn't catch it. That part's a joke. Anyhow, I had a one-time encounter at the Ady's Hotel. It was completely unplanned and unexpected. It was only one time and it meant nothing to either of us. Apparently, less to her than me. It was my first time and it was my only time. I swear to that on my mother's grave."

"Your mother is dead!"

"No, but if she were I would swear on her grave."

"Robert, are you ever serious?"

"I'm sorry. Yes, I am being totally serious now. Once you get to know me, you'll see that I often use humor when making a point because it softens the subject and most people appreciate it as it makes them comfortable."

"Robert, you crazy boy. So, it appears that we are in the same boat. We both have one incident to draw on."

She leaned over and kissed him gently on the lips, and pulled away as he attempted to respond.

"What say we go inside and try for number two together!"

Robert almost broke into a sprint but managed to restrain himself.

They went to Mindy's room.

The next morning, they slept late. Robert awoke to find Mindy sitting beside the bed, staring down at him. She smiled.

He asked, almost hesitant to do so. "How are you this morning?"

As big a smile as Robert had ever seen crossed her

face.

"I am wonderful. I have never felt better in my life. I love my life. Did I ever tell you how much I love life?"

"No, you haven't. Why don't you tell me?" Robert reached over to tickle her ribs and she fell on top of him, laughing and giggling like a school girl.

He had to stop and gaze into her eyes. "Melinda, I have never felt like this in my entire life. How could things be any better than this. It is way too early to say this but here goes. Melinda Francesca Booth, I love you. The moon and all the stars will fall out of the sky before I ever stop loving you. I want to spend my entire life with you and a house full of kids. Stop me before I commit to more than I can provide."

"Robert, admit it, you're just horny and want another roll in the hay!"

"You are so right. You have never uttered a truer statement in your life. How about you?"

"I thought you had to report into your Captain before noon. Isn't that true?"

"Holy smokes, you're right. What time is it? 10:30 already. I've got to get to the court house before noon."

"Tell you what! Let's cuddle for a few minutes and then I'll go to the court house with you and we can show your Captain what you did on your first night of freedom."

"Ha. Okay. We can also show him what I'll be doing for the rest of my time off."

Cuddle, they did. Forty-five minutes later, Robert and Mindy are hustling into the King Street sun on the way to the Martinsburg Court House and Captain Heidel.

31: Back in the Army

Robert was showing Mindy his office, his desk and explaining a little of what his duties are. The door to the inner office swung open and Captain Heidel came out. He noticed Robert and then did a double take when Mindy turned to smile at him.

"Good morning Private. Very good you made it in before the noon deadline. I knew I could count on you. This must be your fiancé that Lt. Robinett was raving about."

Both Robert and Mindy were surprised. Robert because he just found out he had a fiancé and Mindy to find out that Hiram had been raving about her. So maybe, she thought to herself, Hiram is not quite as stoic as he pretends to be. Maybe there is hope for him.

"Thank you, Captain,", said Mindy, playing the role.

"I hope you are not too disappointed."

"No Ma'am, I would say that Lt. Robinett was right on target, so accurate that he could be an Artillery Officer in my company any day!"

"Well, thank you most kindly, Sir. You are quite obviously an officer and a gentleman."

"Private Edwards, I have good news for you although the timing may not be exactly to your liking. You have received orders to report to Camp Averill tomorrow. Apparently General Averill needs a clerk, his non-vet got out. You need to report here at 08:00 to check out, you have to be in Lees Town by dusk."

One of those stars that Robert talked about earlier had just fallen from the sky and hit him directly on the top of his head. He was crushed. He had not really had time to think about what his acquittal meant. Now he knew, he was going back to war. Feeling total despair, he looked to Mindy, who was smiling broadly.

"Robert, that's okay. I must leave in the morning anyway. This is wonderful news. We know where you are going and what you will be doing. I can't think of any General's personal staff killed in the war and you have no reason to be the first. We still have all day and night. We had better hurry back to the hotel so that I can pack. Is there anything else you need from Robert, Captain, before tomorrow morning?"

"No, just make certain to be here by 08:00. You need to see the Pay Master."

Robert saluted the Captain and they were on the way. He asked Mindy if she had a lot of luggage and she replied quickly!

"Nope! Hardly any."

"Then why are we practically running to the hotel?"

"Robert, If I have to tell you, you are obviously more shaken than I imagined."

"I don't reckon that I think as quickly or as ornery as you do."

"Just so you catch up and things will work out fine."

"I suspect I'll catch on and then you will be the one wondering what hit you."

"Well, I hope you study real hard and try your best. I might just hold you to that."

They both simultaneously said, "I love you", turned to each other and laughed.

Robert was absolutely in heaven, heaven on earth, for sure!

After a romantic supper, Robert asked the desk clerk to awaken them at 06:00. He was already awake and up when he received the knock on the door. Mindy was up and sitting in front of the dresser putting her beautiful locks into a tight bun for the trip home.

"Melinda, I want you to know that these couple days have been the happiest days of my life, bar none. I couldn't begin to tell you what they have and do mean to me. If something should happen, in the future, that changes things between us, know that what I am telling you is the absolute truth. I want to spend the rest of my life with you, only you, just you!"

"Are you going to bury your mother again?"

"Ha! No, I'm not going to bury my mom. Just so you know and have no doubt that this is not rushing into anything for me. I have never been more certain of anything in my life. I am madly, wildly in love with you. What do you feel? Tell me before I drop dead from worry."

"Well, Robert, you're okay." She laughed that wonderful laugh and Robert explodes, jumps her and here they go again.

In the middle of the hugging, the kissing, the belly rubbing, the exploring and the adventures, Melinda is totally engaged in telling Robert that he is the man of the hour, the day, the week and so on into infinity. Her world began and will end with him, hopefully in this very position. She pledged to do his dirty laundry, have his children, cook his meals and wipe his butt if he needed it.

It was about this point that it dawned on Robert that she was joking him again.

"Enough, enough, he yelled, I have to concentrate."

They both burst out laughing. Rolling on the bed, they could have easily gone back to sleep. Robert was going to be very close to being late.

Once again, he spent his last day in Martinsburg running up Kings Street to make it on time.

32: Payout and Orders

Robert was directed to the Pay Master's office. It was explained what money he would be receiving.

"Edwards, you have been paid in full through April 1863. Therefore, you are due payment for May 1863 through September 1864, this present month. There was a pay jump in June of this year, changing the Private's pay from $13 a month to $16. If I calculated this correctly, and trust me, I did, you are owed $249. How do you want that?"

"I guess I will take that in cash, Sir. I will place it in a bank for safe keeping. I surely don't want to do that here."

"Not recommended, but cash you want, cash you get. Be careful, that's a lot of money."

"Yes, Sir. I will, Sir. Thank you, Sir."

Robert walked out of the Pay Master's office with more money than he had ever seen in his life.

Captain Heidel let Robert use the court house carriage to take Mindy to the train station. The Captain volunteered to go with him and seemed disappointed when Robert declined, saying he could handle it. Robert found himself thinking he would likely get lots of offers to help with Melinda. That would take some getting used to.

In the carriage, on the way to the train station, Robert pulled over in a quiet shady spot. He took Melinda into his arms and gave her a long soft kiss. Not a sexual kiss, a long deep loving kiss.

"Melinda, I got paid all of my back pay today and I want to ask you a favor. I got $249 in total. I will need some money for getting settled in with my company, not much but a little. If I give you $240, can you keep it as our nest egg so we can start working on our future together?"

"Robert, are you sure you want to do that? That's a lot of money to give someone that you have known for about a month in total. You sure you want to do that?"

"Melinda, we will need that money for our future, our future together. If I were at all worried about trusting you with our money, we wouldn't have a future. Keep this for us and I will send more as I get paid. I don't need much. The army takes care of us. The money is because we are serving our country. You keep it for us. Can you carry it safely back to Baltimore and deposit it in the bank? Set the account up so that I can make an allotment, you have my info and I'll update it as soon as I can at Camp Averill."

This time it was Mindy's turn to show emotion. Tears slowly flowed down her cheeks.

"Why are you crying, sweet girl? What did I say? What did I do?"

"Oh Robert, you have so much to learn. I am so happy. I never imagined that things would work out like this. My father thought I was nuts for coming and throwing myself at you. I hoped but I never dreamed that this could go like it did. I know that I am pretty, and I was guessing that you were attracted to me. While I was taking care of you, I caught you looking a bunch of times.

"What I didn't know was could you help me get over this terrible event that I was afraid might have scarred me for life. I didn't know if I would even like sex, if I could ever love. But one thing I did know was that if someone could help me get well, I wanted it to be you. I fantasized of how it would be, and I wasn't even close. You were so wonderful, so caring, so good at what you were doing. Are you certain you only did it once before? I don't care how many times. You learned well. I would like to thank whoever it was that taught you. Seriously! Don't go getting a big head, but you, it, everything is just unbelievably perfect."

They both were a mess by the time they pulled up to the train station. Things had happened very fast. Their time together had flown bye and now it was over. Hopefully just for now and they would see each other again, soon if they were lucky.

They had discussed Robert's discharge date and they had just a few days' shy of four months before his three-year enlistment would expire. Stay alive, stay healthy and stay in love. That was all that is required and they could live a happy life together, forever. Sounds simple enough. And then the train and Melinda were gone.

33: Active Duty

Robert had heard many things about Brigadier General William W. Averill and he wasn't so sure about this assignment. Averill did not sit back and command. He led from the front.

In December of 1863, Averill raided near Staunton, Virginia, which was General Stonewall Jackson's headquarters. He had bitten off more than he could chew although he had some successes. He was pursued vigorously by Stonewall Jackson. The outcome was the capture of the total Yankee ambulance train, about two hundred prisoners, their horses and equipment, many carbines and revolvers, forty or fifty blacks, eight of Averill's officers, including his Adjutant-General, a Lieutenant-Colonel, Averill's horse, his servant, and many of his maps of fifteen or twenty counties. Jackson also captured many of their mules and wagons, while his own losses were small.

In May of 1864 in battle, Averill was shot in the forehead by a musket ball. It bounced off and cut a gash across his temple with gushes of blood. It was so bad that he had to leave the front, seek out the field surgeon who patched him up, and the General returned to the front and to the fight.

Robert found himself repeating Melinda's words for most of the 22-mile trip on his new steed, which had been procured for him compliments of his new boss. "Stay alive, stay healthy and stay in love." That was all Robert had to do.

Often, in war as in life, plans change. Sometimes they just fall apart. By the time Robert approached Camp Averell, it was no longer Camp Averell. While Robert stood trial in Martinsburg for desertion, Brigadier General Averell was being fired by General Sheridan for not aggressively following his orders.

On September 21-22, Sheridan's army had routed Confederate General Jubal Early at Fisher's Hill. The Rebs had been on the run now for more than a week and Sheridan was determined to end Confederate dominance in the Shenandoah Valley, once and for all.

Sheridan ordered Averell's horse soldiers to stay on their tails but the cavalry had dallied around Fisher's Hill and didn't arrive in Woodstock until midday, eight hours after the Union infantry. Sheridan ordered Averell to close with the enemy immediately. Averell chose instead to bivouac that evening. Upon hearing this decision, Sheridan immediately relieved Averell and replaced him with Colonel William H. Powell, one of his brigade commanders. Averell was ordered back to Wheeling, took sick leave instead and resigned from the Army.

So, by the time Robert rode into camp, it was Camp Powell. He knew absolutely nothing about the Colonel but secretly hoped Powell was not quite as aggressive as Averell had been. Realistically, Colonel Powell was serving on the staff of General Sheridan, therefore complacency was likely not one of his attributes.

Powell was extremely active for the month of October 1864. Under orders to destroy confederate trains and tracks, they traveled in and around Front Royal. They didn't have much success and were called back by Sheridan to support the last major battle in the Shenandoah Valley at Cedar Glen near Strasberg, Virginia.

While Robert didn't fight, he was in constant

motion, keeping up with Powell and the fast-moving cavalry. In early October, General Sheridan had been called to Washington by the Secretary of War for a military conference. Col. Powell and his troopers were camped at Belle Grove Plantation at Cedar Creek, enjoying the break in what had been a busy and extremely tiring month of non-stop action.

Confederate General Jubal Early had been very aggressive in the Shenandoah Valley, taking his troops as close as 5 miles to Washington and creating havoc in the capital.

Union General Grant had put General Philip Sheridan in charge of 32,000 seasoned Union troops in the newly formed Army of the Shenandoah. Their success in turning the Shenandoah Valley into a barren waste caused a desperate tactic by Early to attack the Union Army at Cedar Creek. On the early morning of October 19th, the Rebs had complete surprise on their side and the rout of the Union forces was in full force. Had Early not paused to give his soldiers a rest, history well could have been changed in total. However, he chose a break in the action. That gave Sheridan, returning from Washington, the opportunity to rally his troops who had been on the run. He regrouped, charged and they totally defeated the Rebels who were never a force to be reckoned with again in the Shenandoah Valley.

This amazing turn of defeat into a rousing victory likely won re-election for President Lincoln. Lincoln was leading a demoralized country, and was being pushed at home to end this war and give into the Rebs demands for peace talks. It gave Americans hope that they were right and they could win. While Gettysburg had turned the tide, the Battle of Cedar Creek likely won the war for the North.

Sheridan's Ride was celebrated world-wide and made *Little Phil* famous, a fame he enjoyed the rest of his life.

For the remainder of Robert's time with Colonel Powell and the Army, they continued to execute Grant's orders for what is known to this day as *The Burning*. Destroying more than 1400 barns of hay, confiscating all stock, securing all blacks to prevent further planting, the Army of the Shenandoah destroyed everything in its path, 70 miles long by 30 miles wide. The valley would no longer support southern troops and basically ended all military resistance in the area. The south would never recover.

34: A Free Man for a Short Time

On January 24, 1865, Robert H. Edwards was released from the Army. Given the option of transportation, he selected the train to Washington. Having corresponded with Melinda on a regular basis, she knew his release date and eagerly anticipated their reunion.

It was evening in Washington when the train pulled into the station. Lights along the platform in front made lighted areas and dim areas. As Robert stepped down from the train, he was unable to recognize anyone. His initial disappointment made him wonder if Melinda had received his wire. Wild negative thoughts rushed to the surface. Had she changed her mind? Had something happened? Oh, please Lord, please let her be okay.

When Melinda stepped from the shadows, an

elderly man and a young boy were with her.

Robert spotted her and suddenly, he was running. "You're here! Thank God you are here!"

Melinda's smile said "Yes, I am here!" They embraced and they kissed and they kissed and they embraced. Finally, stopping to catch their breath, Robert acknowledged that they were not alone.

"Mr. Booth, Jacob, I'm sorry for this terrible display. I was so afraid that your daughter had come to her senses and didn't show up. I'm afraid that I didn't see anyone but her." Robert extended his hand and Mr. Booth grasp it firmly.

"Young man, Mindy was the same way and has been for a week or more. Hopefully now, she can return to her senses and be normal again."

"Father, you're not supposed to tell Robert that I was crazy waiting for him to arrive! I'm the one supposed to be in charge in this relationship."

"Oh, Ha! Believe me, Sir, she is in charge. I just want to be with her, take care of her, hopefully for the rest of our lives."

Hugging each other again, they happily stared into each other's eyes. Robert said: "Thank you for being here. I was so afraid."

"I was afraid too. I feared that now that you had your freedom, you would take the opportunity to go home to Ohio and forget all about me."

"Melinda, I am here to find a job and then ask your father for your hand in marriage. I already have a recommendation from Colonel Powell and a possible job at a local hospital as a clerk with the possibility of getting into the medical field."

"You can ask my father whenever you like but you better ask me right now."

"Really? Now?"

"I don't want to wait any longer. I don't want any doubt. I want to hear it now, Edwards, and I want to hear it from you."

Robert laughed. He dropped to one knee on the platform on the train station in Washington D.C. He had been in town approximately twenty minutes and he was proposing to the first lady he met.

"Don't be laughing, Robert. This is serious stuff."

"I told you before that I use humor to make serious situations easier to handle. So, here goes. Melinda Francesca Booth, most beautiful girl in the world, would you do me the honor of being my partner through life? Would you let me love you more than anyone else in the world ever has and make you happier than you have ever been before. If you will say yes to becoming my wife, I promise every day to make it better than the day before and leave you with no doubt ever that you made the right choice. Melinda, sweet Melinda, will you marry me?"

Tears ran down Melinda's cheeks and her shoulders trembled. She had not blinked once during Robert's request. She lowered her head, appeared to struggle to regain her composure. She slowly raised her head and her beautiful blue eyes, as soft as Robert had ever seen them, locked directly on his.

"Oh, yes, darling Robert, oh yes!"

35: Job Hunting

Thus, on January 24, 1865 Robert H. Edwards had survived the war, was honorably discharged from the 1st WVA Cavalry, and became engaged to Melinda F. Booth. Not a bad first day for a civilian.

On the Monday following, Robert set out to find a job. The past week had been wonderful. He had virtually spent every minute of each day with the woman he loved and had not experienced one wavering minute where he thought he might be rushing into something he didn't want. Things, life in general, never felt so right as it did at this moment in his life. Based on Melinda's actions and words, there was no reason to think that she felt anything but the same. Life was good, so now, he needed a job.

With his reference letter in hand from Colonel

Powell, he headed to Armory Square on the Mall Hospital.

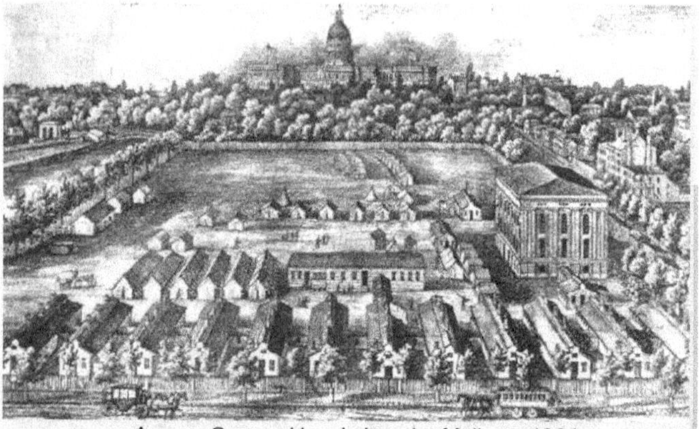

Armory Square Hospital on the Mall, ca. 1864

Source: www.archives.gov

Inquiring at what he assumed was the Information Desk at this huge hospital, Robert asked where he might find Doctor Maxwell Surge. Informed that the doctor was making his rounds, he was directed to the doctor's office, where he waited in the outer office, which contained one desk, multiple chairs, and was empty of people.

Robert had been sitting for perhaps an hour when a middle-aged man in a white jacket and a bit older heavy-set woman dressed as a nurse came in. The assumed to be doctor looked tired and the nurse appeared grumpy.

The man asked Robert what he needed and Robert introduced himself and explained he had a reference letter from Colonel Powell. The doctor's eyes sparkled and he asked, "You know my brother-in-law?"

Robert replied, "If you mean Colonel Powell, then, yes, I know your brother-in-law. I served with him in the Shenandoah Valley campaign. I was his clerk!"

The doctor introduced himself and he and Robert shared questions and answers. Finally, when they were satisfied that they were talking to the right person, Doctor Surge asked what he could do for Robert.

Robert replied, "I have been out a week and I need a job so that I can stay in Washington and get married." The moment the words left his mouth, he realized how silly they sounded.

The doctor chuckled. "Do you have anyone in particular in mind? There are a lot of eligible women in this town looking for a man!"

"Yes Sir, I do have someone in particular and I want to get married before she comes to her senses. Right now, she wants to marry me as well."

"Why that is great! Says here that you were Bill's clerk and that you had also clerked for a Brigadier

General."

"Yes Sir, General Stahel. Until he was relieved of command before Gettysburg."

"And you are a wounded vet. That's commendable as well! Can you still stomach working with the military?"

"Yes Sir, in fact, I would surely enjoy it and I like helping folks who need it. I hated seeing the lives lost and destroyed and would love to help make things better for those who need the assistance."

"Well, Edwards, I don't know if you are just blowing smoke, but I need a clerk and am willing to give you a chance to prove yourself. Things are hectic here but I don't know if it is any worse than being on the battle line trying to keep up with a Cavalry Officer."

"Sir, thank you and I will take the job gladly. My future wife will probably want to know how much I am going to be paid, for planning purposes."

"Ha, I understand that completely. I'm married as well. The job pays $800 annual, which is just about the going rate in Washington."

"Thank you, Sir, that is better than I expected. When do you want me to start?"

"Today is fine, if you can. Nurse Hudgins will take

you to the admin office and get your paperwork started. She will also be the person showing you the job since she has been dual hatted since Emery, the last clerk, passed."

"I'm sorry to hear that. What happened to Emery?"

"Consumption got him. He held on as long as he could, because he knew he was dying. I hope we get this disease under control here soon. There is some promising research going on, I just wish they could hurry."

"Okay, enough talking. This is Nurse Hudgins. You will be working for her for the next few months. Her orders are my orders. Keep her happy and I'm happy. Good luck, Robert and welcome to Armory Square Hospital."

So, Robert had a job. He wanted to rush out and find Melinda and let her know. The first day stretched to ten hours and it was late by the time he got back to his newly rented boarding house at 451 Massachusetts Avenue. He decided, as he ate his supper, that he would likely have to wait until the weekend to notify her of his success. He would be better equipped to tell her what the job entailed by then.

36: Lee Surrenders and Lincoln Is Murdered

April 9, 1865, Lee is trapped and surrenders at Appomattox Court House, Virginia. Once the troops in the field get the word, the war is over. The Union military finds itself facing the overwhelming tasks of transitioning from war to a peace time environment. Determinations as to how many troops to maintain, what would their role be in the immediate reconstruction effort, and as important, getting the no longer needed veterans out of the service. These men needed to be released quickly so they could get home where they can begin the arduous task of rebuilding their lives and the American economy. The U.S. has been focused on winning the war. The manufacturing efforts were centered on providing the military essentials to accomplish this effort. Things needed to change, to get back to normal, and the U.S. had to catch up with the rest of the industrialized world.

Chaos! Fear! Mourning! Blame! John Wilkes Booth shoots the President of the United States on the 12th of April in Ford's Theatre. General Grant and his wife had been scheduled to attend but backed out at the last moment. Grant was additionally a target for Booth's assassins. Imagine the ramifications had Grant been in attendance and killed as well. Would that have been enough to rally the South into a second effort? Civil War historians have often argued this point.

Source: www.archives.gov

The world-famous actor Edwin Booth was quick to come out condemning his younger brother and history declares that the murderer's name was never spoken within the Booth family again. Some people were quick to assume that any Booth should share the blame for this atrocious act. Robert was very worried about Melinda and her family's safety. Melinda had just received permission from her father to move into Robert's boarding house but there were concerns for her well-being. Robert was working long hours clerking at the hospital and there would be many times that she would be alone. When he approached Melinda with his fears, she would not consider moving back home with her father.

"Robert, I have left home and I am set on building our lives together from this point forward."

"Melinda, I understand your feelings and agree totally. However, sometimes circumstances change and we must have the ability and good sense to change our plans when necessary. I work such long hours and you will spend so much time alone that I will fear for your well-being."

"Radicals are not mad at me, Robert. They are mad at the Booth name. The simple solution is that we need to change my name to Edwards."

"Now? I thought you wanted to get married in Chauncey so that you could meet my family and see what you're really getting into."

"Robert, you just said yourself that circumstances call for a new plan. We can still do that later, but getting married now will resolve this situation and we are only stepping it up a few months. Plus, my father will be much happier if we go ahead and make this living arrangement legal."

"Melinda, I don't know if I will ever think and act at your speed. You amaze me with your abilities and I just hope and pray that you don't grow bored with me."

"Robert, I promise to you now and forever that I will spend every day working to make you the happiest man alive."

"Sweet girl, you already have!"

On Monday, the first day of May 1865, a memorial observance took place in Charleston, South Carolina. During the war, more than 250 union soldiers had died during captivity while incarcerated at the Hampton Park Race Course in Charleston. More than 10,000 black freedmen, including preachers, teachers, and

3,000 school children enrolled in freedmen's schools participated in the memorial service. The freedmen spent the day cleaning and landscaping the unmarked graves of the dead union soldiers who had died while trying to right America's wrong.

On this same Monday, Robert H. Edwards and Melinda Francesca Booth stood in front of a Justice of the Peace in Washington D.C., exchanged vows and became husband and wife. Two individuals stood with them. Lieutenant Hiram Robinett and Wilburn Booth.

37: Hiram is Reassigned

About this same time, Hiram had been notified that the 22nd VRC was being re-assigned to Camp Chase in Columbus, Ohio in June. Although not thrilled to be leaving the Washington-area, Hiram decided that this was the opportune time to visit home, family, and the 40 acres of land he had purchased in February. Located outside of Chauncey, Hiram knew that it was a good investment and that likely, one day he would go home for good. He requested a seven-day leave of absence which was approved and on the last day of May, Hiram hopped the train to Marietta.

The morning of the June 8, 1865, Hiram reported for duty at Camp Chase. Every third day, he was responsible for the guard details, reporting issues and resolution of those problems within his purview. On the 21st of July, he was assigned collateral duty as the Acting Assistant Inspector General. Hiram continued this routine for the remainder of the Summer and Fall.

The Army, the 22nd VRC and Camp Chase were heavily involved in the process of discharging Union soldiers and releasing Rebel prisoners. Thousands of non-vet soldiers were arriving at Camp Chase to be processed for discharge. They had to be paid and any debts settled for money owed the government. This took time and personnel to handle the administrative workload. The hours were long, the soldiers were tired, anxious and very impatient. It was hard work and it kept the staff very busy.

On the 29th day of July 1866, Hiram received a telegram from his father that his young cousin Stineman had passed away from camp dysentery. He had been discharged after spending a good amount of time in the brigade hospital and not recovering sufficiently to perform his duties. A similar illness had ended the musician duties of Stineman's younger brother Charles as well, but he had finally recovered. Hiram applied but couldn't get the time off to go home for the services.

Finally, the workload was manageable and members of the VRC were being sent home as well. At the end of the year, Hiram was released and required to muster by mail until further notice.

Before leaving Columbus, Hiram visited Ohio Congressman Tobias A. Plants to inquire about positions that were available with the Bureau of Refugees, Freedmen and Abandoned Lands (Freedmen's Bureau) in Washington D.C. These were highly politically-influenced positions, requiring nomination and appointment from political powers within a state. Hiram applied for a clerk position. The Freedmen's Bureau was under the War Department and provisions were made to consider former military for the positions. Hiram was technically still on active duty, so it was easier to get him approved but it still took some time.

Hiram went home to Chauncey and his new home, built by his father and friends and neighbors. The house was short of grand but was two stories, had a big front porch and a barn under construction. At his insistence, Ezekiel and Jane, Charlotte, Moses, Kate, Warren and William had moved in. There was more than enough room and it was obvious that they were all enjoying the new homestead.

Weather permitting, Hiram enjoyed working on his property and found himself thinking that once he had conquered the world, or at least his world, he might come back here and settle down. Not yet, but one day.

Hiram visited Nye Cemetery and his mother's grave, marked only by flowers. In front of her grave, young cousin Stineman was laid to rest. He had a temporary wooden cross in place until his government-provided tombstone arrived. Hiram reflected that when he died, this location would be fine with him.

38: Melinda with Child

Melinda was with child. She had been working with Robert as a volunteer at the hospital. This allowed them to see each other during the day, eat lunch together when possible, and made things easier.

Robert could not be happier. He was going to be a father along with the most beautiful mother in the world. Things were going well at home, although they would need a bigger place soon. Work also was going extremely well. As the Doctor's clerk and the Nurse's whipping boy, he was learning so much. His bosses were impressed and surprised with the ease in which he picked up the medical terms. So was he. Transcribing everything that the Doctor diagnosed, prescribed, described, and documented gave a real inside view about what a physician faced daily. Robert found it all interesting and felt a great deal of satisfaction with the support and aid the doctor gave to so many soldiers and veterans.

By the end of the year, Robert had decided to inquire of the doctor how he could become more involved, learn more and perhaps train to become a physician.

Melinda was extremely excited to see Robert's progress and the changes that were taking place in him. It was apparent, at least to her, that he was maturing, gaining confidence in himself and his capabilities. Each day, she felt certain that things were going to work out fine and she was happy.

39: Freedmen's Bureau

By February 1866, Hiram had received his appointment approval and reported to work at the Freedmen's Bureau. Being still in the service, he was able to retain his rank and military pay, and this was the best of two worlds as far as Hiram was concerned.

Hiram worked in the office of the Director, General Oliver Otis Howard, a Medal of Honor winner during the war. Howard, from Maine, before the war had planned to be a man of the cloth and was known as *The Christian General.* His appointment by Lincoln to head the Freedmen's Bureau was very appropriate because of his background plus his compassion for his fellow man.

In June 1866, Hiram was discharged from the Army and his pay became $1200 annual. As one could imagine, clerking would have been an incredibly challenging job at the bureau, based on workload alone. A letter to his father, written in January 1867, depicts the job and the challenges the staff faced every day.

Freedmen's Bureau circa 1866-1867. Source: National Archives

Hiram's letter to his father Ezekiel...

Sunday, January 6, 1867
Washington D. C.

Dear Father,

Just returned from church and thought I would take a few minutes to let you know how things are progressing. Most of the events will, of course, be concerning my work, because that is mostly how I spend my time.

I did spend yesterday afternoon with Robert, although I will confess, it was not a very productive adventure for either of us, as we spent it in a local tavern drinking beer. I am certain that you are shocked, knowing my distain for alcoholic beverages. However, I console myself with the logic that the pressure of my job likely forced this once in a great while encounter with the dark side of life. Robert would use a similar excuse as the schedule that he keeps in his medical studies would challenge any man's sanity as well as his physical wellbeing. He works long hours at the hospital and no one is more surprised than I am as to the drive he continues to demonstrate. His marriage to Mindy has changed him, certainly for the better. He is maturing and although I miss the old wild and free Robert, I really like this new fellow.

I love my job at the Freedmen's Bureau. The tasks that General Howard and the Staff tackle every day would wear out most ordinary men and I am solidly convinced that these men are far from ordinary. Their dedication is only surpassed by their vision and their unwavering loyalty to more than four million freed colored people who will never know them or fully appreciate their efforts.

Of course, as you know, much of my time as a clerk is spent obtaining information, putting it in a useable order, seeking approval from the appropriate office, publishing the finished product with the appropriate number of copies and ensuring that the proper distribution occurs. The best part of the job is absorbing the data that I am manipulating, which is incredibly interesting and educational for me.

I don't want to bore you or concern you with the environment that our agents face daily in attempting to accomplish their jobs. The anger of the common citizens often boils over and people lose control of their senses and their humanity. The hatred, not too strong a word, is everywhere. Northerners are very shocked and upset as to how this post rebellion environment is working out. Southerners and ex-Rebels are bitter and continue to take it out on the public every chance they get. The poor colored folks are in danger most every minute of every day and the existing laws make it nearly impossible to protect them.

The procurement efforts that I am involved in to assist the school start-ups are monumental. Our office handles most of the effort for all 15 areas because the funding comes through HQ, which is just down the hall. Planning and execution is in place for more than 800 schools and it is estimated to be more than 1,000 before we finish.

Imagine the frustration and horror we all feel when we hear the stories of agents, teachers and students being harassed, beaten, tarred and feathered, run out of town and one even murdered. The existing laws designed to protect the freedmen are ineffective and would be comical if the situations were not of a life-threatening nature. Colored people must have a credible white witness before a Judge can prosecute any of these thugs and ruffians. What white person is going to stand up for a colored person when they end up in the same or more danger themselves once identified? The Judges appear to be intimidated themselves and are refusing to prosecute most cases.

President Johnson is doing all he can to disrupt the success of the Bureau. He has had several agents dismissed and it is rumored to be because of their enthusiasm towards doing what we were hired to do. It is a well-known fact that the President doesn't like General Howard or the Freedmen's Bureau. It especially irritates him that Lincoln and Congress put it under the War Department, which makes it difficult for him to control, even as Commander in Chief.

Father, I apologize for bending your ear in this manner. Note that it is probably the beer talking and I should be better by tomorrow. I can indeed ensure you that this won't become a habit, nor will Mindy allow Robert to lead me astray too often. As an aside, if I ever find a girl like her, I will snatch her up in a minute.

So much has changed in just four short years. For certain, these four years have been the fullest they could possibly be, seeming both endless and flying by. Moments of excitement, chaos, outright fear, and the disgust of death, all mingled with these amazing feelings of incredible accomplishments. Life in Chauncey

Ohio and growing up on the farm seems like such a long time ago. I realistically do not see me returning permanently to Chauncey any time soon. There is so much more to see and do.

I hope everyone is well. I see Athens, Chauncey, and Nelsonville in the news often and they each appear to be a booming metropolis. Let's hope that keeps up and that life continues to treat you well. Tell everyone hello for me, tell them to write and I will do my best to answer each individually. I am always busy but never too busy for family.

Your loving son,

Hiram

40: Reconstruction Resistance

The Ku Klux Klan was growing in power and in performing atrocious acts. They terrorized blacks, agents, teachers and the few supporters the freedmen had. Anything that could be done to impede the success of the Freedmen's Bureau was a direct blow to civil rights of the freed black families. This period of reconstruction of the southern states and the efforts to induce failure was indeed the darkest period in American history, far darker than the Rebellion. Southern Americans who are proud of the actions of their ancestors during this era obviously do not know or refuse to recognize the true shame associated with their disgraceful behavior during this period of our history.

Hiram and the other employees of the Freedmen's Bureau knew that their positions of employment were temporary. Funding was becoming an issue and the associated politics continued to become worse by the day. President Johnson was doing everything he could to appease his southern constituents and the former rebels were doing everything they could to return the South to its former glory, mostly at the expense of the blacks.

So, it would be natural that Hiram and the other clerks associated with the Freedmen's Bureau would be pursuing future opportunities. One option was going back on active duty with the US Army, in the Veterans Reserve Corps.

Section 4 of the Bureau of Refugees, Freedmen, and Abandoned Lands Act provided the opportunity for any veteran working for the Bureau to stay on active duty. For most, this would be both an advantage and an opportunity. It was an advantage as it made the associated benefits of being active duty available, especially free medical care. It provided opportunity for better positions and promotions, and a career in the U.S. Army.

Therefore, mid-summer 1867, Hiram began the process of applying for an active duty position in the Regular Army.

Request for Return to Active Duty
Washington D.C.
June 21, 1867

Hon. E.M Stanton
Secretary of War,
Washington D.C.

Sir,

I have the honor to apply for a Commission in one of the Veteran Reserve Corps Regiments of the United States Army.

I enclose herewith for your consideration testimonials from Officers under whom I have served and others who know me. Also, a brief statement of my services rendered the Government during the late Rebellion.

Hoping this may receive your favorable consideration,

I have the honor to be
Very respectfully, Your Obedient servant
Hiram Robinett

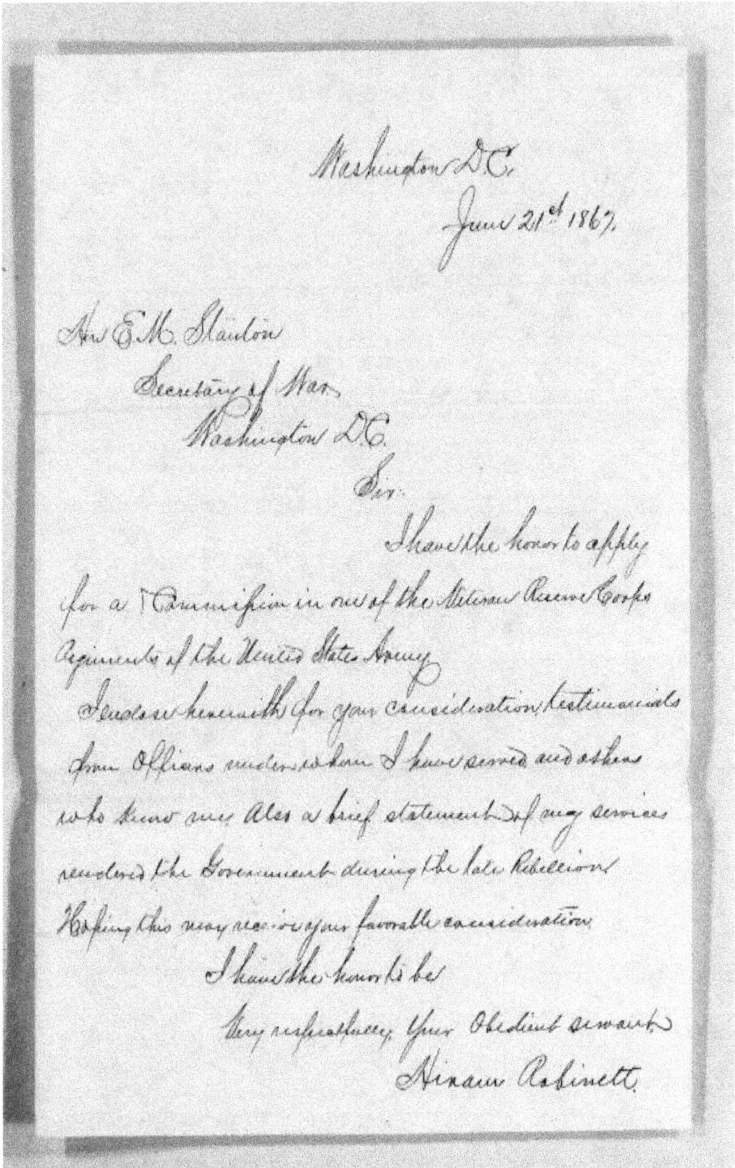

Washington D.C.
June 21st 1867.

Hon E. M. Stanton
Secretary of War
Washington D.C.
Sir:

I have the honor to apply for a Commission in one of the Veteran Reserve Corps Regiments of the United States Army.

I enclose herewith for your consideration testimonials from Officers under whom I have served and others who know me. Also a brief statement of my services rendered the Government during the late Rebellion.

Hoping this may receive your favorable consideration

I have the honor to be
Very respectfully, Your Obedient servant
Hiram Robinett.

Source: www.archives.org

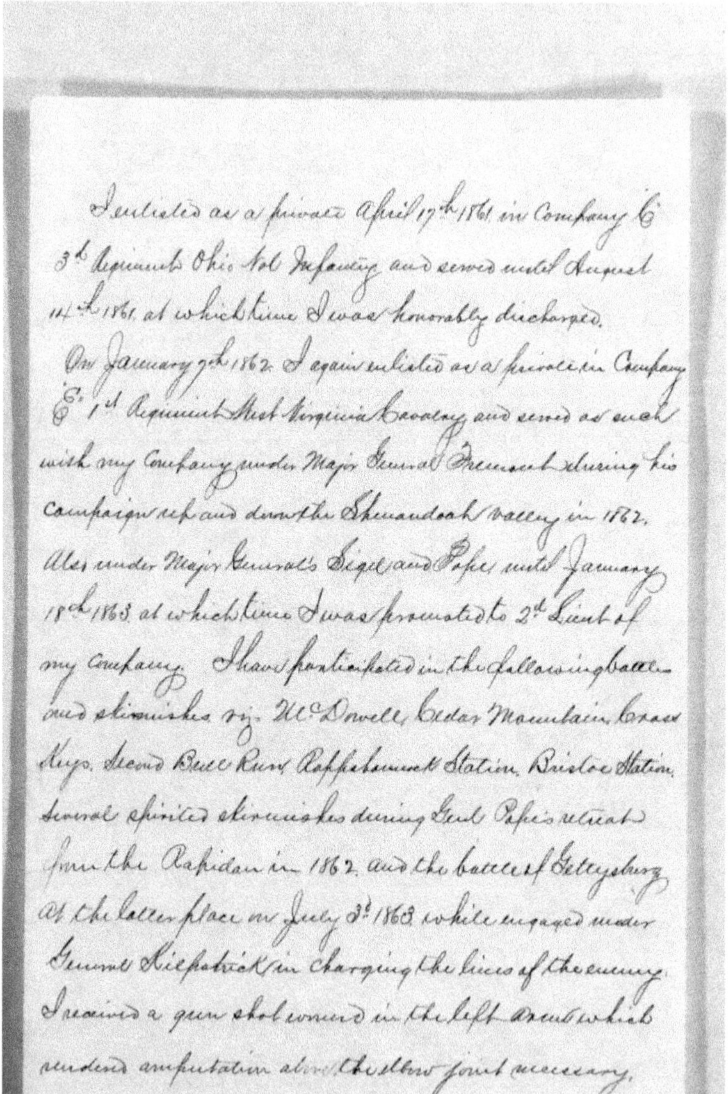

I enlisted as a private April 17th 1861 in Company C 3d Regiment Ohio Vol Infantry and served until August 14th 1861 at which time I was honorably discharged.
On January 7th 1862 I again enlisted as a private in Company E 1st Regiment West Virginia Cavalry and served as such with my Company under Major General Fremont during his campaign up and down the Shenandoah valley in 1862. Also under Major General's Sigel and Pope until January 18th 1863 at which time I was promoted to 2d Lieut of my Company. I have participated in the following battles and skirmishes viz: McDowell, Cedar Mountain, Cross Keys, Second Bull Run, Rappahannock Station, Bristoe Station, several spirited skirmishes during Genl Pope's retreat from the Rapidan in 1862 and the battle of Gettysburg. At the latter place on July 3d 1863 while engaged under General Kilpatrick in charging the lines of the enemy I received a gun shot wound in the left arm which rendered amputation above the elbow joint necessary.

Source: www.archives.gov

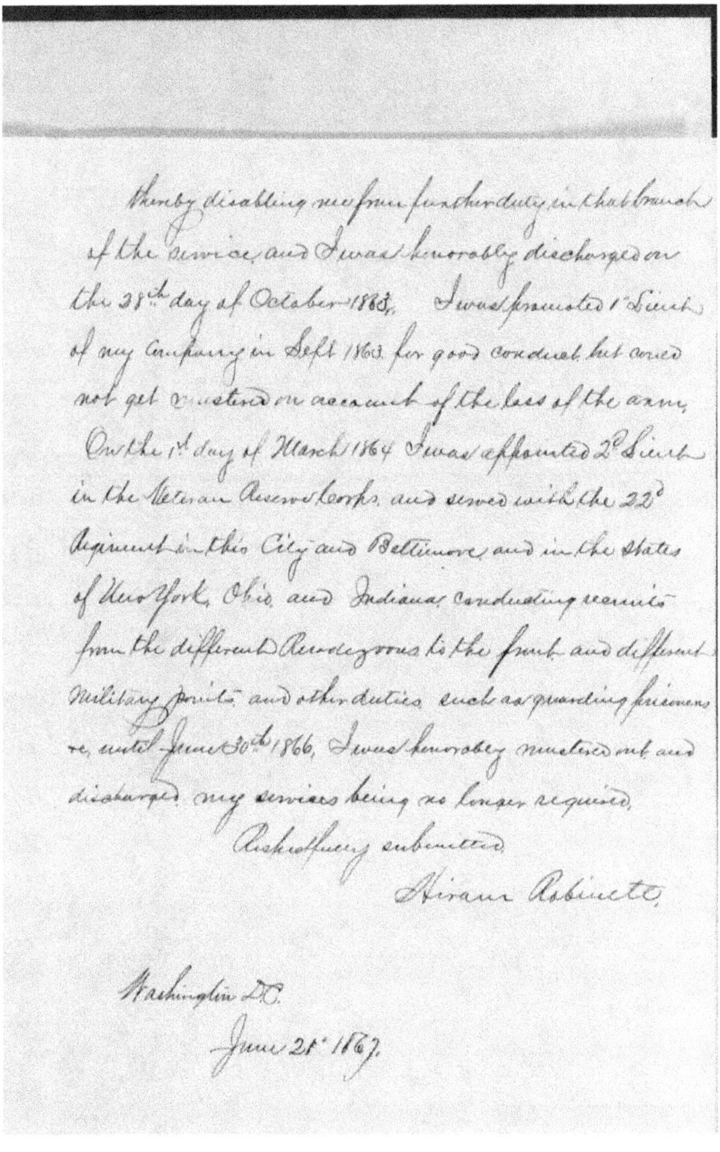

thereby disabling me from further duty in that branch of the service and I was honorably discharged on the 28th day of October 1863. I was promoted 1st Lieut of my Company in Sept 1863 for good conduct but could not get mustered on account of the loss of the arm. On the 1st day of March 1864 I was appointed 2d Lieut in the Veteran Reserve Corps, and served with the 22d Regiment in this City and Baltimore, and in the States of New York, Ohio, and Indiana, conducting recruits from the different Rendezvous to the front and different Military points, and other duties such as guarding prisoners &c, until June 30th 1866, I was honorably mustered out and discharged, my services being no longer required.

Respectfully submitted

Hiram Robinett

Washington D.C.

June 21st 1867.

Source: www.archives.gov

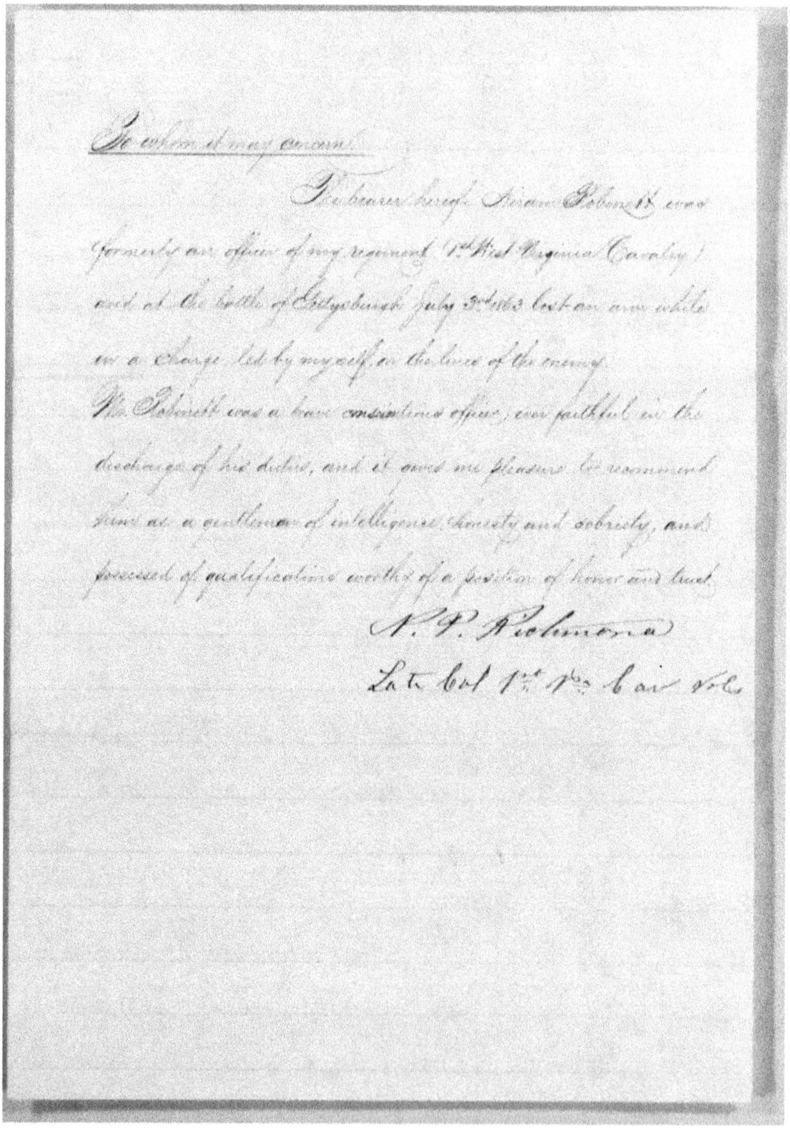

To whom it may concern

The bearer hereof Hiram Robinett was formerly an officer of my regiment (1st West Virginia Cavalry) and at the battle of Gettysburgh July 3rd 1863 lost an arm while in a charge led by myself on the lines of the enemy.

Mr Robinett was a brave conscientious officer, ever faithful in the discharge of his duties, and it gives me pleasure to recommend him as a gentleman of intelligence, honesty and sobriety, and possessed of qualifications worthy of a position of honor and trust.

N. P. Richmond

Late Col 1st Va Cav Vols

Source: www. archives.gov

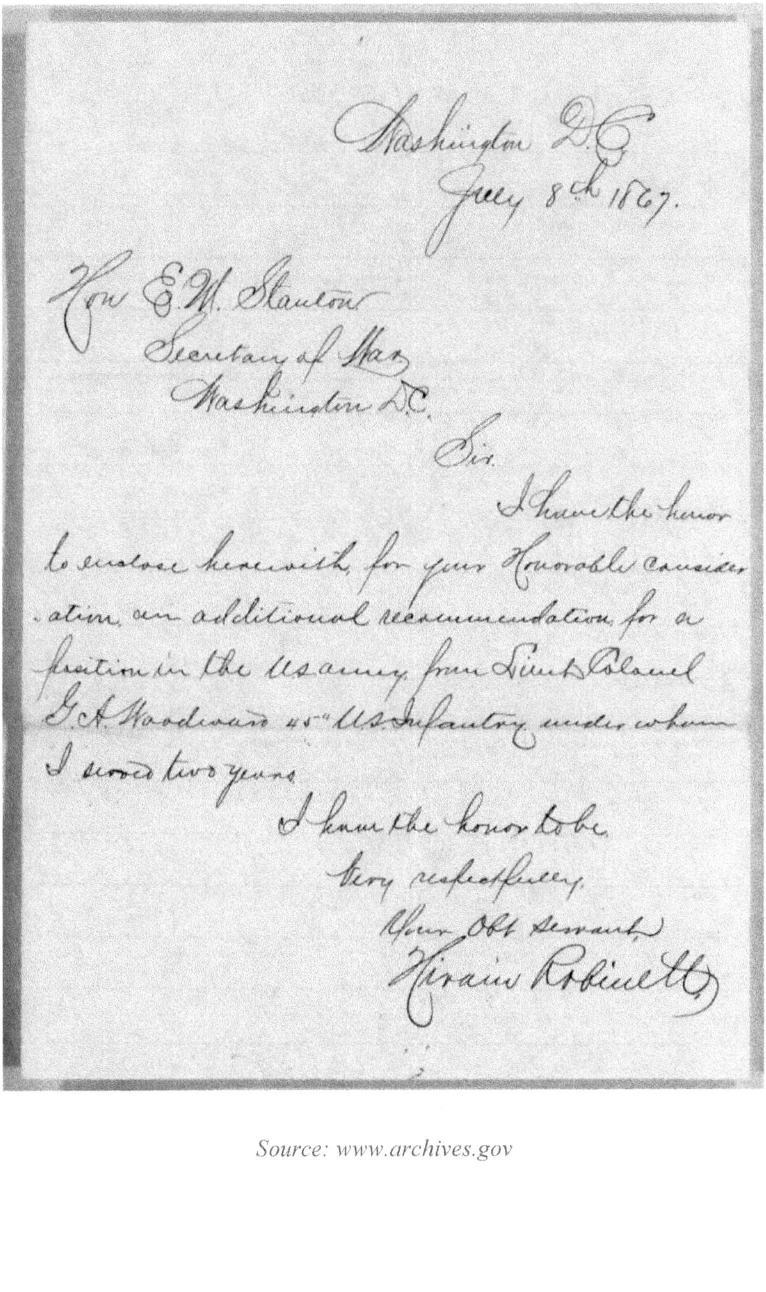

Washington D.C.
July 8th 1867.

Hon E.M. Stanton
Secretary of War
Washington D.C.

Sir.

I have the honor to enclose herewith, for your Honorable consideration, an additional recommendation for a position in the US army from Lieut Colonel G.A. Woodward 45th US Infantry under whom I served two years.

I have the honor to be
Very respectfully,
Your Obt Servant,
Hiram Robinett

Source: www.archives.gov

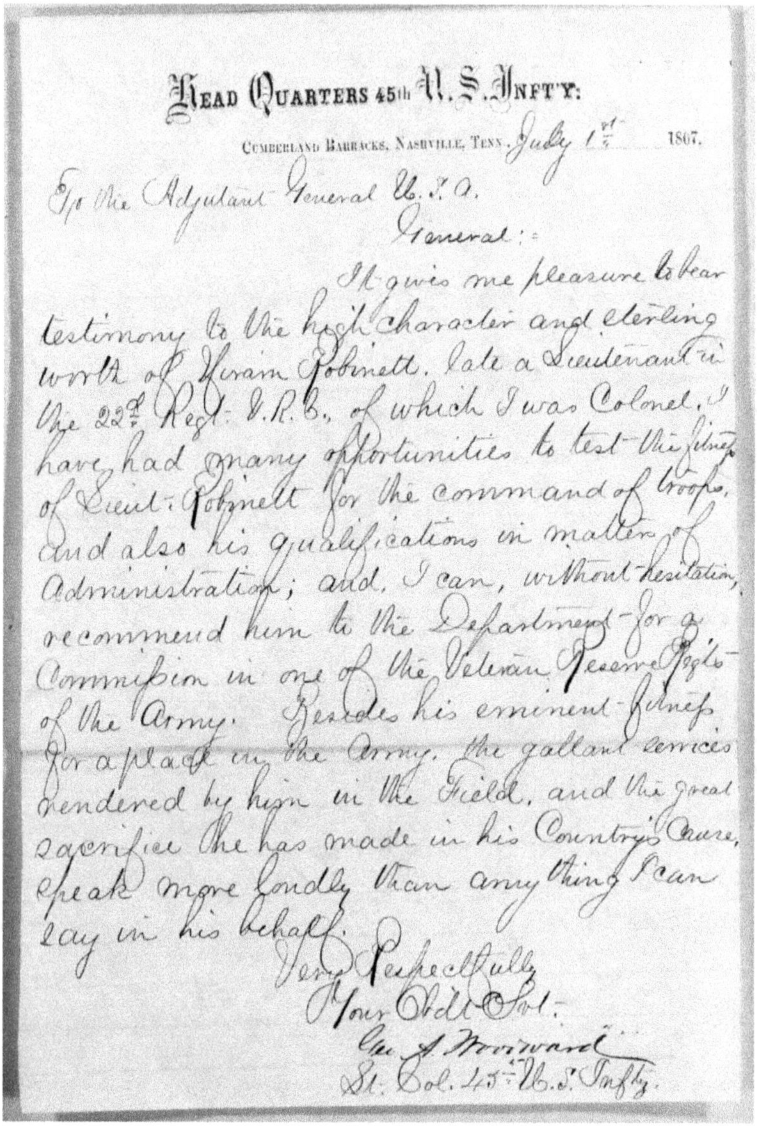

HEAD QUARTERS 45th U.S. INFT'Y:

CUMBERLAND BARRACKS, NASHVILLE, TENN. July 1st 1867.

To the Adjutant General U.S.A.

General:-

It gives me pleasure to bear testimony to the high character and sterling worth of Hiram Robinett, late a Lieutenant in the 22d Regt. V.R.C., of which I was Colonel. I have had many opportunities to test the fitness of Lieut. Robinett for the command of troops, and also his qualifications in matter of Administration; and, I can, without hesitation, recommend him to the Department for a Commission in one of the Veteran Reserve Regts of the Army. Besides his eminent fitness for a place in the Army, the gallant services rendered by him in the Field, and the great sacrifice he has made in his Country's Cause, speak more fondly than anything I can say in his behalf.

Very Respectfully
Your Obdt Svt.
Geo. A. Woodward
Lt. Col. 45th U.S. Infty.

Source: www.archives.gov

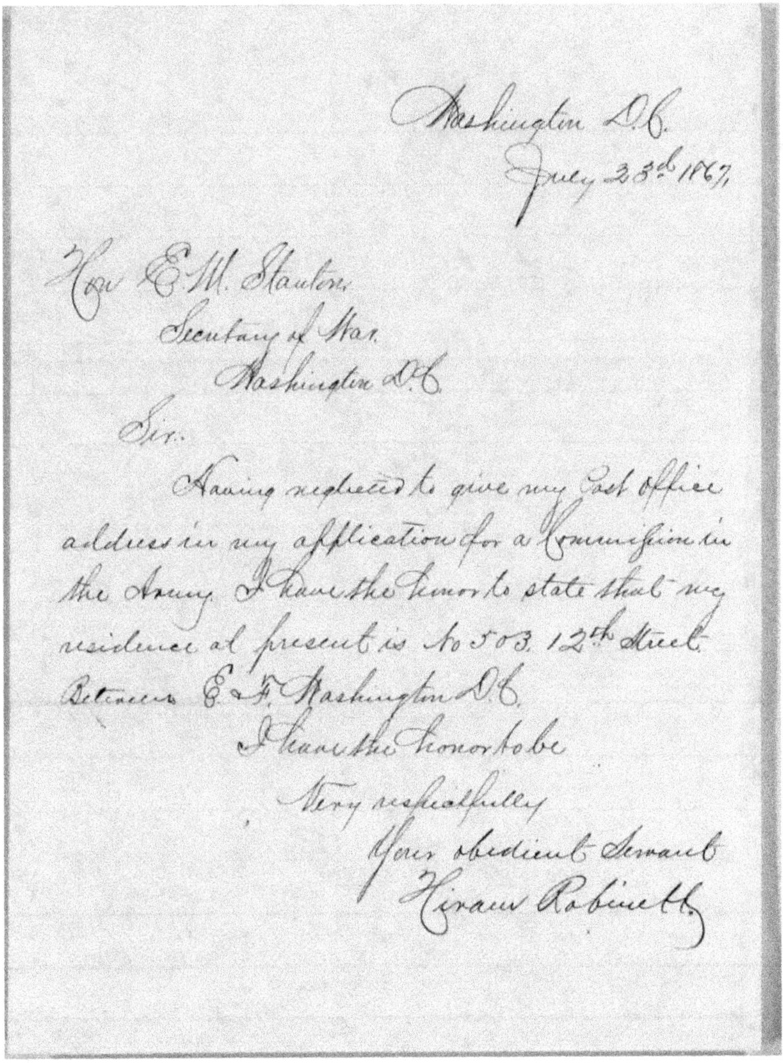

Washington D.C.
July 23rd 1867.

Hon E.M. Stanton
Secretary of War
Washington D.C.

Sir.

Having neglected to give my Post Office address in my application for a Commission in the Army I have the honor to state that my residence at present is No 503. 12th Street Between E & F. Washington D.C.

I have the honor to be
Very respectfully
Your obedient Servant
Hiram Robinett

Source: www.archives.gov

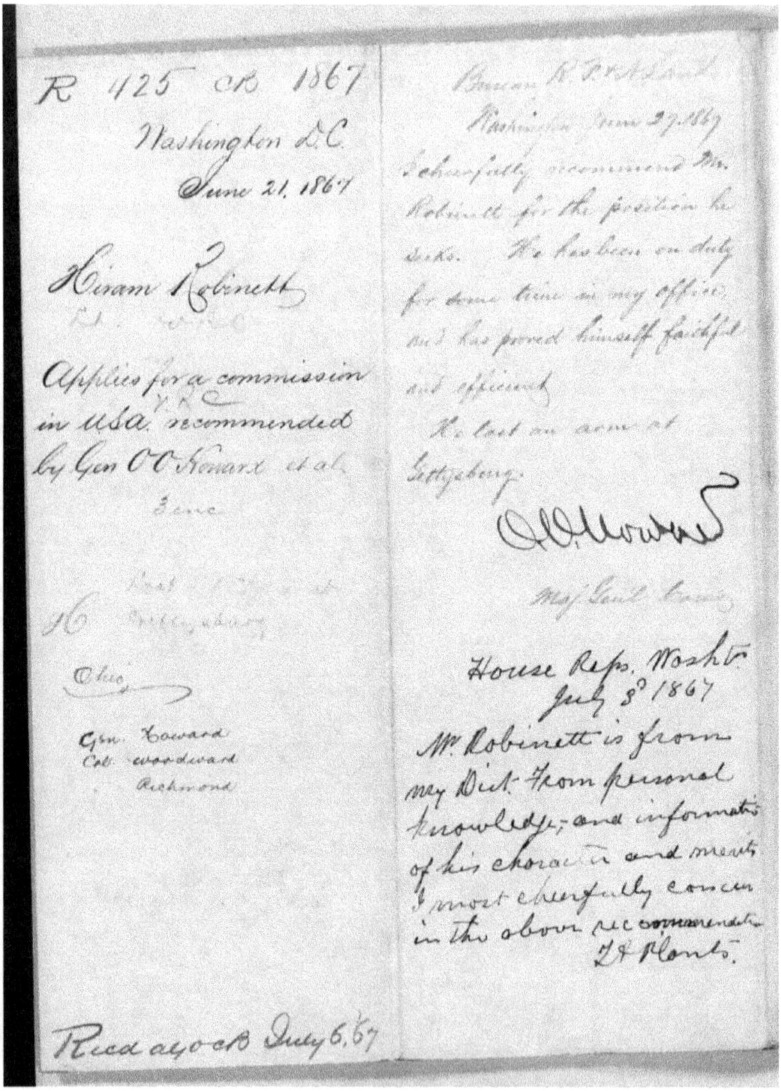

R 425 CB 1867

Washington D.C.
June 21, 1867

Hiram Robinett

Applies for a commission in U.S.A. V.R.C. recommended by Gen O O Howard et al.

Ohio

Gen. Howard
Col. Woodward
Richmond

Rec'd A.G.O. C.B. July 6, '67

Bureau R. F. & A. Lands
Washington June 27, 1867

I cheerfully recommend Mr. Robinett for the position he seeks. He has been on duty for some time in my office and has proved himself faithful and efficient.

He lost an arm at Gettysburg.

O. O. Howard
Maj Genl. Comy

House Reps. Washtn
July 3rd 1867

Mr. Robinett is from my Dist. From personal knowledge, and information of his character and merits I most cheerfully concur in the above recommendation

T A Plants.

Source: www.archives.gov

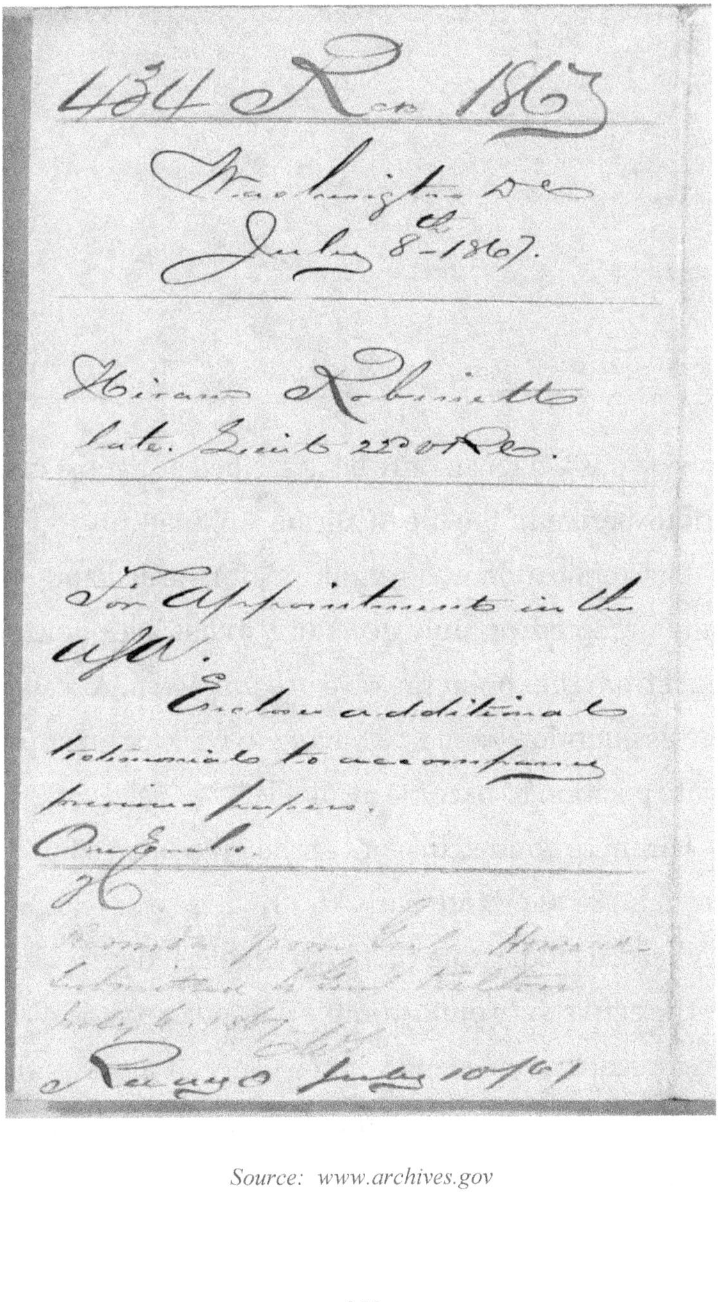

434 R. 1867

Washington DC
July 8th 1867.

Hiram Robinett
late Lieut 22nd O.V.I.

For Appointment in the U.S.A.
Encloses additional testimonials to accompany previous papers.
One Encl.

H

[illegible]

Recd July 10/67

Source: www.archives.gov

41: Hiram's Final Battle

Now begins what can only be described as a most mysterious period in the life of Hiram Robinett.

His application was submitted, forwarded and officially accepted on July 10, 1867. What actions were taken from that point forward are unknown. A reasonable assumption would be having to wait for an appropriate position to become available.

Hiram continued to work at the Freedmen's Bureau through 1867 and into early 1868. There exist no military records indicating that he was selected or rejected for the active duty opportunity. Without a physical record indicating one choice or the other, it appears that no action was taken. Hiram didn't pull his application, as again, there would be correspondence to indicate his decision.

Hiram's letter to his father, Ezekiel...

Friday, 21 February 1868

Washington D.C.

Dear Father,

I wanted to let you know that I will be coming home the first of the month for a brief stay. I have been struggling of late with some health issues that I feel certain are temporary.

Doctor Surge, who is the Head Physician that Robert works with, insists that I need to get some rest if I ever expect to get well. Robert put it in terms that I was more likely to understand. He likened it to someone who burns the candle at both ends, of which I admit I am guilty, eventually burns their wick off. I believe my wick is fine but do agree that these past two months, the illness has really put a damper on my productivity at work.

I have missed more than a week of work this month and that is totally contrary to my beliefs and my performance history. I do my fair share and believe in a full day's work for a day's pay. My friends and coworkers have noticed my struggles and done so much to help me that it indeed embarrasses me and yes, shames me as well. I need to get well and back on the job and if it takes some recuperation time, then that is what I must do.

I would stay in Washington if I could find someone to tend to my needs, but Robert insists that I need to be around family and in a friendly environment to conquer this thing and get back on my feet. His absurdity goes to the point that he has arranged to take a leave of absence and accompany me on the trip home. He is bringing Melinda and their baby girl with them. I ask him for assurances that his trip has been approved and that he is not deserting, which he did not find all that amusing.

So, please let me know if you can accommodate my visit without too many inconveniences. It shouldn't be long and I can basically care for myself. It will be nice to be home and see how you are doing on the farm. Spending time with Charlotte and Mose is something I have not done in a long time and I look forward to seeing everyone.

I assume that Robert has informed his folks but you know him as well as I do, so you might mention our visit to them.

Looking forward to seeing you
Your loving son,
Hiram

The next known fact concerning Hiram is sadly on his death bed. He is home, just outside of Chauncey, Athens County, Ohio. He is scribbling his name on a hastily put together will, leaving most of his earthly goods to his father, Ezekiel.

In the name of the Benevolent father of all
I Hiram Robinett of Dover township Athens County
and State of Ohio do make and publish this my
will and testament

Item 1st. I give and devise to my beloved Father
Ezekiel Robinett all of the farm on which he now
resides situate in Dover township Athens County Ohio
containing about forty [illegible] acres of land more or less
during his and my step Mothers natural lifetimes
and all the Stock and Household goods of every
kind belonging to me. also I give [illegible] devise to
my father Ezekiel Robinett all [illegible] hand or may
come to hand now due me or ma[illegible] due hereafter

Item 2d. I devise and bequeath to my Brother Moses
Robinett my watch

Item 3d. I devise that at the death of my father and Step
mother that the property above devised to my father and
Step Mother be equally divided between my brother
Moses Robinett and my sister Charlott Robinett

In testimony hereof I have hereunto set my hand and
seal this 24th day of March A.D. 1868.

Signed & acknowledged by
Hiram Robinett as his last
will & testament in our
presents & signed by us in
his presents

A. L. Bright
N. M. Edwards

Hiram Robinett (Seal)

Hiram's illness really devastated Robert and hurt Melinda as well. His health deteriorated so rapidly and while not totally unexpected was extremely difficult to accept. All the symptoms of consumption took place so rapidly that Robert or Doctor Bright could do nothing to make him comfortable. Robert tried to spend as much time with Hiram as he could but the point was reached where Hiram was delirious, in and out of consciousness and his wonderful, adventurous life was abandoning him.

Robert was sitting at the dinner table with Ezekiel, Jane, and Melinda who was breastfeeding baby Roberta. Doctor Bright came in from the bedroom and told Robert that Hiram wanted to talk with him. Robert inquired as to how he was doing and the doctor slowly shook his head.

Robert hurried in and sat beside the bed. He took Hiram's hand in his and asked, "Hey Buddy, how you doing?" He could tell by the look in his friend's eyes that it wouldn't be long. Hiram was dying and Robert's heart was breaking.

"Robert, you have been my friend my entire life. There is no one on the face of this earth that I care more for that you. I have always tried to be there for you and the biggest fear that I have in dying is that I won't be there for you next time. For that, I am so sorry."

Tears were running down Robert's cheeks and he indeed thought that he might just die before Hiram. "Hiram, you have always been there for me. All through our childhood, all through the Army, you are always there. Without you, I wouldn't have Melinda. Without you, we wouldn't have our sweet baby girl.

I don't know if I have ever said it to you but I know that you know and have always known that you are my hero, who I always wanted to be, and that I have and always will love you."

Through the tears, Robert saw that the life in Hiram's eyes had gone. He was lost. Robert didn't notice when and immediately wondered, did he even hear what I said. Once again, as always, Hiram held the last card and had the last say.

Letter from Ezekiel to General Howard...

Bureau of Refugees, Freedmen, & Abandoned Lands
District of Columbia
Attn: General O.O. Howard

March 26, 1868

Dear General Howard,

I felt an obligation to my son, Hiram Robinett, to inform you that he passed on Tuesday, March 24th. With Pastor S. H. Bingman conducting the services, our family and my boy's childhood friends said good-bye to our wonderful warrior. Hiram was laid to rest in the Robinett Family Plot in Nye Cemetery beside his loving mother, Lucinda, and directly behind his young cousin, Private Stineman Robinett.

I am certain that in your position of authority that you receive such notices almost daily and I feel certain that one cannot be more special to you than the many others that you have lost. Please understand that Hiram was special to us and you were very special to him.

As you know, Hiram was an officer in the West Virginia 1st Cavalry and suffered a debilitating injury at Gettysburg that could have ended his military career. Hiram's love of his country and his exuberant enthusiasm to serve overrode the pain and discomfort that he constantly endured. When he was permitted to return to active duty in the Volunteer Reserve Corps, he could not have been happier. Given the opportunity to spend much of his duties in the Baltimore and Washington City area excited him and fulfilled his emotional drive to contribute.

After his release from active duty a second time, as you know, he worked in your office performing what he considered was the ultimate job – helping to rebuild our great nation. He was inspired by your leadership and your personal accomplishments and he spoke of his admiration for you openly and without embarrassment. He liked to believe and told me often that he would succeed like you and I have no doubt in my fatherly mind that he would have. I believe he was destined for great things and I am likely the only one who believed it even more assuredly than he.

Now, by fate or whatever power greater than Hiram, he will not have the opportunities to continue his quest. I fear that one of his last thoughts was some disappointment. I pray that was not the case. As his father, I could not be prouder. His accomplishments, his dedication to excelling at whatever he did, and his love of family and his country, is enough for me now. Sadly, it must be.

Take care of yourself, General. So many in this country are depending on your efforts and your success. Hiram admired you and knew you would heal our nation. You have our support.

Respectfully Yours,
Ezekiel Robinett
Chauncey Road, Chauncey
Athens County, Ohio, USA

DEATHS.

ROBINNETT.—Died at Chancey, Athens county, Ohio, on March 26th, Mr. Hiram Robinett, of Consumption.

Lieutenant Robinett was among the first to enter the army from this county, having enlisted under the first call for three months' volunteers, as a private in the 3d Ohio Infantry. He afterward enlisted in Company E, 1st West Virginia Cavalry, was promoted to a 2d Lieutenancy, and lost an arm at Gettysburg.

For the past two years he has been engaged in the office of General O. O. Howard, Commissioner of R. R. F. and A. L., at Washington, D. C. where he has gained many friends. Lieutenant Robinett leaves a large circle of friends and acquaintances, whojmourn, with his relatives, his early death. "He has fought the good fight," may he rest in peace.

The Athens Messenger, April 1, 1868

The above obituary is actual of the time. The following obituary was created after the fact and while not totally accurate, contains a synopsis of his time with the 1st

West Virginia Cavalry.

Hiram Robinett Obit, Waterloo, Athens County, Ohio, USA, 24 Mar 1868

Birth: 1843
Death: Mar. 24, 1868

HIRAM ROBINETT(E), 2nd LIEUT.
Hiram Robinett was born on 31 January 1843 in Waterloo Twp, Athens County, Ohio. Company "E" First W. Virginia Cavalry January 7, 1862 he joined the Virginia Mounted Volunteers as a Private. This organization subsequently became the West Virginia Cavalry where Hiram served in Company E, First Regiment. He enlisted for 3 years in Clarksburg, as indicated on his muster sheets. Hiram was promoted 1 March 1862 to Quartermaster Sergeant and then was promoted to 2nd LT. on Jan 18, 1863. Wounded in action at Gettysburg on July 3, 1863, "the wound aforesaid was received in line of duty and while nobly battling for the Flag of his country." Shot through the left elbow causing arm to be amputated the following morning by Surgeon Capehart of the First Virginia Cavalry. Spent some time recuperating in the hospital at Hanover, Pennsylvania. Discharged on Surgeons Certificate of Disability on October 28, 1863. Hiram died on March 24, 1868. Single. 24 years, 3 months, 25 days old. Place of death - Dover Twp

Burial:
Nye Cemetery
Chauncey
Athens County
Ohio, USA

Source: www.ancestry.com

Letter from General Howard to Ezekiel...

Bureau of Refugees, Freedmen, & Abandoned Lands
District of Columbia
Major General O.O. Howard

June 13, 1868

Dear Mr. Robinett,

It was with great sadness that I received notice via your letter of the passing of your son, Lieutenant Robinett. While it is true that I have lost many brave warriors during my time in the service of our country, I have been fortunate during my tenure here at the Bureau. We who managed to make it through the terrible four years of war have certainly enjoyed this assignment. The comforts associated with working in an office, getting regular meals three times a day and sleeping indoors in a real bed are a few of the things we will never take for granted again.

While this Washington office is large, we have all spent many hours together working towards successfully supporting 4 million freed human beings. Working the required time to accomplish this monumental effort has provided the benefit of getting to know my staff quite well. We have had many meetings, formal and informal and I was given the opportunity to get to know your son, Hiram.

Hiram was a very sincere and honest young man. He did his work thoroughly and was always ready to help where ever needed. I know him to be a church going practicing Christian who loved his God openly and proudly. Hiram was funny and fun to be around, but always knew when the fun stopped and the work began. He was loved and respected by his fellow clerks and the Senior Staff. He was often asked for by name when someone needed assistance.

I am likely rambling on here, but I want you to understand that we, like you, felt Lieutenant Robinett was a cut above and we respected him greatly. We will miss him and commit to his honor our continued efforts to finish this job in the manner that he would expect. I have been notified and have personally contributed to a fund to provide a graveside monument to your son. You need not apply for a headstone as we are taking care of that for you.

We, of course, realize that nothing can replace Hiram for you or your family. Please find some comfort in God's reverence that your son fought the good fight and made a difference. Man can ask for little more.

Respectfully,

O.O. Howard

Major General, U.S. Army

Brigadier General Oliver Otis Howard.

Source: www.britannica.com

42: A Final Service

The tombstone arrived from Washington DC to Athens on June 29, 1868. Ezekiel made the arrangements to have it placed on Hiram's grave on July 3rd, the anniversary of Farnsworth's Charge at Gettysburg. With the family, the Edwards family including Robert and his new bride, Melinda, and Mrs. Susan Knowles, widow of Sidney, attended.

Once again, Pastor Bingham spoke of Hiram's qualities, accomplishments and unfulfilled dreams. He described the provided stone and what it demonstrated about the American character, the friends of Hiram's in Washington, and how they felt about this young man from Chauncey. He read General Howard's response back to Ezekiel and that was an emotional moment for

Hiram's tombstone. Nye Cemetery, Chauncey, Ohio

all. The gathering was much more upbeat this second time and there was a great presence of pride, not only for Hiram but for Sidney, Robert, his Uncles John and Curtis, cousins Stineman and Charles, for all the other casualties from Chauncey and for everyone in attendance who had suffered through this difficult time in

American history. As the service was ending on this bright beautiful summer day, several dark clouds blew in to remind folks that while the war had ended, the reasons behind these terrible times did indeed still exist. Hiram and Sidney and the 650,000 other men and boys had not died in vain. They had preserved the Union and that was all they could do. Those who remained faced a long battle of their own to finish the job.

Hiram's tombstone inscription...

Lt. Hiram Robinett, son of E. + L. Robinett.
Died March 24, 1868. Aged 25 y 3m 24 d. of the
1st VA. C + I.R.C.

Left side:
"No farther seek his merits to disclose,
Or draw his frailties from their dread abode,
There they alike in trembling hope repose,
The bosom of his Father and his God."
Thomas Gray
The Epitaph, St. 3.
Elegy Written in a Country Churchyard (1750)

Right side:
"Erected by his Friends and Associates in Washington as a token of their high esteem for his many virtues."

43: Life Goes On

Robert and Melinda had decisions to make. He had been studying under Doctor Surge for two years and felt that he was likely as ready as he would ever be to start his own practice. He wrote a letter, tore it up and instead sent a telegram asking for Doctor Surge's advice and consent to follow his dream, here in Ohio.

Melinda was very excited about staying in Southeastern Ohio when compared to Washington D.C. Both the Edwards family and Hiram's family made her feel very comfortable and she felt this would be a great place to raise Roberta and however many more children came along.

She was very sad to lose Hiram as well, but she knew that he wouldn't have stayed around long anyway. He had bigger and better things to do and that would have been wonderful for him. However, she had made the right choice. Robert was the one for her. His demeanor and his loving personality was more than she would ever be able to absorb in one lifetime, and she was going to make her best effort to keep him happy.

Three days later, Robert's father came hustling into the house with a telegram response from Doctor Surge. Robert read aloud that the Doctor was more than happy to endorse Robert and claimed that even Nurse Hudgins approved.

William and Melinda both vigorously applauded. Melinda asked, "May I be the first one to kiss Doctor Robert H. Edwards?" and jumped him before he could reply. Through the kiss, Robert mumbled, "Yes, yes, yes!" as his father shook his hand.

So, Robert began his search for a good location to open his practice. What he hoped for was a growing community that wasn't overly saturated with physicians. While there were many towns and villages that would appreciate another doctor, the population had to be large enough that Robert could support his soon-to-be growing family.

44: Zaleski It Is!

In the 1850s, Zaleski, in Vinton County, Ohio had been a grand experiment. Investors from Great Britain banked on found coal to be the opportunity to get ahead of the game and the industry by building a community that would provide the foundation for the riches they hoped to garner in the growing coal industry. They built the roads, a grand hotel, an iron furnace, encouraged railroad investment for a piece of the action and waited for success. Unfortunately, the coal that they had hoped would be a part of the Hocking Vein was not. Instead of anthracite (hard coal), it proved to be bituminous (soft coal). While it was fine for domestic use, it would not burn hot enough for industrial purposes. High volume sales were not to be.

Zaleski only had one doctor in 1868, so this is where

Robert decided to open his practice. He moved his family into a comfortable home on the main road and set up his office in the front of the two-story house and Melinda set about making a home in the back half and the upstairs.

While residents weren't beating his door down, he slowly established a customer base and a reputation of being the young doctor down the road. Melinda initially served as his nurse and they both performed the necessary clerking duties. They made a good team and people seemed to like the two of them and the practice grew.

They worked hard and sometimes odd hours but Melinda somehow had ample time to spend with Roberta, who was walking and beginning to require more attention. The week of Thanksgiving 1868, Melinda discovered that she was again with child.

Both she and Robert were thrilled but realized that she would not be able to keep up the effort required to be the receptionist, nurse and a mother. She found a young woman from their church who wanted to become a mid-wife, and she became Doctor Edwards' new assistant. Her name was Joy Ann Six and they found out that she was a niece of Moses Six who was married to Hiram's sister Nancy. The saying of a small world seemed especially true in southeastern Ohio.

In late January 1869, they received a letter from Melinda's father. He declared that he would like to come visit them for a month or so. Melinda's brother had signed on to be a teamster and was headed west. Wilburn said that he just couldn't handle the farm by himself and that he didn't want to. He was tired of farming. He decided, if it was okay with them, that he would come out, look around and if he liked Ohio, find him a place, maybe in town.

Melinda couldn't think of a better possibility and her excitement alone made Robert's agreement easy. Her dad would come live with them and stay if he wanted to.

Wilburn being there helped make life easier for them all. He was able and very capable of maintaining things plus kept the outside of the house looking good. He was popular around town and became one of the fixtures on the bench under the big oak in the center of town. There were four regulars, two of them elderly like 'Wil' as he became known. The fourth, Leroy Bennett was a Civil War vet who took one too many musket balls to his hip and hobbled around with a cane. He also carried a rubber ball in his hand that he squeezed to keep the circulation flowing in his limbs. Leroy was full of stories and opinions that he loved to share or use to stir up a fuss if things got boring. They rarely did but that didn't seem to bother Leroy.

A healthy baby boy was born on the 8th of July 1869. Robert insisted that he be named Hiram and Melinda agreed to his wishes and Robert Hiram Edwards was christened into the Presbyterian Church two weeks later.

45: Worn Out

The middle of August was extremely hot. It was truly the dog days of summer. Robert was tired and he couldn't seem to shake these doldrums regardless of what he tried. Melinda had noticed that his appetite wasn't up to his usual standards and therefore, he was losing some body mass.

This continued well into September. Some days were better than others, but there were fewer and fewer tolerable days. Finally, Melinda had enough and she went for a walk one Monday morning and returned with old Doctor Hollister, the town's other physician. Robert knew exactly what this was all about and he said, "Good morning, Doctor, how are you this fine morning?"

"Better than you, obviously! Your wife tells me that

you haven't been feeling well, not eating, losing weight and haven't done anything about it. She said that I am going to examine you and that she has enough rope to hog tie you, if necessary."

"I would love to tell you that she is exaggerating but I'm afraid that not the case." Turning to Melinda and Joy, Robert continues, "would you ladies excuse us for a few minutes?"

Robert could see the concern in Melinda's eyes, but she conceded to his wishes and tugged Joy's arm as they left the room.

Doctor Hollister did as thorough an exam as possible, with the limitations that they faced in 1869. Consisting mainly of questions, they talked about Robert's symptoms, what he had tried thus far and if he noticed any relief or changes. Hollister was also interested in who he had been treating and what their problems were; and importantly, who he had been treating when he began experiencing his symptoms.

Doctor Hollister asked, "Have you been treating anyone with Phthisis?"

"Consumption? Not recently. In fact, since I opened my practice, I have not. I treated a few people in Washington but haven't seen any since my friend died a year ago March."

Hollister continued, "In the Boston Medical Journal, there's an article by a French Scientist who has demonstrated that consumption is contagious. He also believes that most of us carry the virus in our bodies but it only creates problems when certain conditions are met. Being physically run down appears to be one of the contributing factors, which of course, leads to other problems which only are magnified as your body tries to fight this debilitating disease."

Robert was familiar with the great majority of the information the doctor was sharing with him. But now, he was on the other end of the stick. He was the patient. He was the sick one. He wasn't the one poking the stick, he was the one being poked and it didn't feel so good. He found himself wishing he had learned this earlier. Relating to the patient's feelings and fears paints a totally different picture and it wasn't a picture Robert cared for. He made a note in his mind to be more considerate when diagnosing someone, to show more compassion.

Doctor Hollister and Robert agreed to meet again on Wednesday morning to discuss their approach to treating Robert's condition.

Melinda entered the room after the doctor had departed. The look on her face almost brought Robert to tears, as he already felt like crying. Without saying a word, she laid her head on his shoulder and hugged him firmly. Neither spoke for several moments and finally Melinda stepped back, locked those beautiful blue eyes on his, and asked "Well, what are we facing?"

At that moment, Robert knew that she and the children would be fine.

46: The Sun Comes Up

As the sun rose on a chilly Wednesday morning, the 10th of November 1869, the main street in Zaleski was quiet, deserted. Doctor Hollister had been gone several hours, Wilburn was stirring around in the kitchen, hopefully making coffee. Melinda had sat and watched the night disappear and the sun come up.

She had lots of things to think about. She had cried all the tears that she had to cry. Roberta and little "Hie" had to be taken care of. She found herself so wishing that they had been here, but knew that it was for the best and their safety that they were not. It was fortunate that William and Sophronia had so graciously taken the kids while she and Robert fought this battle. This fight that they knew they couldn't win. Melinda knew in her heart that they didn't lose. They just didn't win.

Her sweet Robert would be laid to rest in a cemetery in Athens, not in Nye Cemetery, not with Hiram. She understood that the Edwards family was planning on moving to Athens and that Robert would be close and they could visit him often. That was appropriate. Cemeteries are not for the deceased; they are for the living, to grieve.

Melinda and her father had talked this through and there wasn't anything to keep them here. Between them, they decided that they might like moving back to Gettysburg. Wilburn grew up in that area, and it was home to him. Melinda, because that is where she was born, where she had thought her childhood was ruined and where she found her Sir Lancelot, her knight in shining armor. In the back of her father's wagon.

Wilburn softly opened the storm door and handed Melinda a full cup of coffee. She invited him out and he settled on the old bench beside her rocking chair.

They sat for a while, not saying a word. Melinda took a long drink of the warm coffee, looked over at her father and said, "When Robert proposed to me, he said he wanted to spend the rest of his life with me. Somehow, I thought it would be longer." Melinda lowered her head, sat very still for several minutes. Her father bent towards her to see if she was crying. She wasn't.

Mindy raised her head and looked past the morning sun. She uttered: "Okay. So, what's next?" Wilburn didn't respond. He knew Melinda wasn't talking to him.

The End

About the Author

Curt J Robinette is a career Navy man, including 27 years as a Navy contractor in Information Technology. An interest in family history led to the discovery of his grandfather's brother Hiram who served as a cavalryman in the Civil War. Twenty plus years of continuing discovery of interesting information led to a perceived obligation to tell Hiram's story. Golfing, bowling and drinking beer fell by the wayside in the effort to 'get 'er done'. Curt is also the editor of *The NEW Nelsonville Tribune* which is a Facebook page dedicated to memories of growing up in our hometown of Nelsonville, Ohio. Twenty-two hundred participating members contribute to a weekly published (but not printed) newspaper. Work has additionally begun on a second novel involving Hiram's family and living in southeastern Ohio in the 1800s.

Notes

This novel is based on historical facts and many assumptions by the author were necessary for the holes that existed between the facts. Most personal correspondence (italicized for recognition purposes) was created as fiction by this author. The other included documents are copies of historical letters or actual government documents.

Hiram and his family members are real. The military events associated with Hiram did occur, his reactions, comments, etc. are basically what I believe he would have done, saw and said in response.

Robert H. Edwards and his parents are real as well. Robert is as much fact as fiction as far as his military career is concerned. He was Hiram's childhood friend and they did enlist together. Robert was a clerk for several Brigadier Generals. He was accused of desertion at Gettysburg, and he was arrested in Towson, Maryland. He was in jail in Baltimore, Washington D.C. and finally Martinsburg, West Virginia. Robert was court martialed and he was exonerated of all charges and was honorably discharged three months later in January 1865.

Information discovered after the writing of this novel shows that Robert H. Edwards, of Chauncey, Ohio, (our guy) attended and graduated from Georgetown University, School of Medicine, Class of June 1868. He married in Washington D.C. and opened his practice in Zaleski, Ohio. Robert lived a short time and died of consumption on November 22, 1869. Both Hiram and Robert died at 25 years of age.

It should be obvious that details of Robert's adventures are fictional. Every effort was made to use my military logic in deciding how and why he got into the desertion situation and just as importantly, how he managed to get out of it, unscathed and with his reputation intact.

Melinda Booth is my dream girl as she is totally fictional and perfect in my eyes. Her father, Wilburn Booth, fictional as well, is exactly who he had to be. He was strong, capable of being rowed to the point of violence, but otherwise, a quiet and understanding father-figure.

---

[1] Robinet, Robinett, Robinette, Robnet. Spelling varies among families and amongst legal documents, i.e. census data. Often discovered multiple spellings in the same document. Genealogical research has authenticated this line of the family.

[2] Research Brief, Tony Fuller. Robinett Family Association of America.

[3] In the 1850 and 1860 Census, the daughter of William Gibson and Jane Swift Gibson is recorded as Catherine Gibson, born in 1848. In the 1870 Census, she is recorded as Katherine Gibson, born 1848. In the 1880 Census, she is now recorded as Kate Davis, the same name that she used when she married Reuben Davis on December 12, 1872. Her death certificate and probate documents state Kate Davis, as well.

It was a common practice for census takers to spell the names as best they could. Some would ask for the spelling, but most would use whatever version they preferred. Obviously, the name on her marriage certificate would have been of her choosing, so to me, she used Kate from that point forward in her short life. She died in her thirties and Kate Davis is the name on her tombstone.

She obviously liked Kate, so I made all changes to project Katherine. It could have just as easily been Kathryn but the census taker in 1870 wins.

4 Everett, Lawrence. Ghosts, Spirits, and Legends of Southeastern Ohio. Haverford, PA: Infinity Publishing, 2002. pp. 27-29.

5 West Virginia vs. Virginia. The state of Virginia voted to secede from the Union on April 16, 1861. Meeting since February 13th of that year, the state could not come to a unanimous decision. The western portion of Virginia, which was made up in majority by miners and farmers of crops other than cotton, wanted the state to stay in the Union. They were not involved in growing cotton or supporting slavery, plus did not believe that the eastern portion of the state paid their fair amount of taxes based on their revenue.

Thus, Virginia had decided on a wait-and-see approach. The decision to secede was made for them when Abraham Lincoln ordered federal troops to attack Fort Sumter, South Carolina. Virginia quickly opted to secede to help a sister southern state protect and defend states' rights.

As was expected, not all of Virginia agreed with the decision. Northern Virginia, that was snuggled up close and personal to Washington DC, was against secession. Many people in Western Virginia had fought secession from the beginning of the Virginia Convention in February. Therefore, in the eyes of Lincoln and the Federal Government, western Virginia became the state of Virginia and senators and representatives to congress were appointed.

In November 1861, a Secessionist Convention was held in Wheeling and western Virginia began the process of rejecting the state of Virginia's decision to secede. The process was grueling and met with a great deal of concern, anger and criticism from the states' residents. It would take until June 20, 1863, at which time West Virginia became the 35th state of these United States of America.

The 1st (West) Virginia Volunteer Cavalry Regiment served in the Union Army during the American Civil War. It was organized in Wheeling, Clarksburg, and Morgantown in western Virginia (now West Virginia) between July 10 and November 25, 1861. About one third of the members of the regiment were from what is now West Virginia, especially Wheeling. Others were from Pennsylvania, Ohio, and the northern section of Virginia. The unit was originally called the *1st Regiment of Loyal Virginia Volunteer Cavalry* until the state of West Virginia was created in 1863. Most civil war records were modified to reflect the name bestowed, once West Virginia became a state. However, some records such as Robert's Arrest Record, the Unit is listed as 1st Virginia. Bottom line, the names are referring to Hiram and Robert's regiment.

The Virginia Volunteer Cavalry (or any other such designation in this novel) became the 1st West Virginia Cavalry as of June 20, 1863. The historical documents will remain unaltered.

[6] Sidney Knowles was a dry goods merchant in Hockingport, Ohio before the war. He entered as a Private and immediately was chosen to perform as a 2nd Lieutenant in Company E, 1st (West) Virginia Cavalry and Regimental Adjutant. Promoted again just before Gettysburg, he died from a gunshot wound direct to the forehead in Farnsworth's Charge on the 3rd day of battle. His wife, Susan, had to sell the business and lived off Sidney's small pension and what she could make in Nelsonville, Ohio as a seamstress. She raised two boys

---

and never remarried. Susan passed away in Nelsonville on February 7, 1917.

7 Robert meets Belle Boyd, who is historically acknowledged to be a Confederate spy. Internet article "Belle Boyd, Cleopatra of the Secession", demonstrates that her actions during this created scenario are totally in line with her genuine character. Historically, the time table doesn't fit exactly but this author suggests that it makes for a better story.

Belle Boyd

Isabella Marie Boyd, best known as Belle Boyd, as well as Cleopatra of the Secession and Siren of the Shenandoah, was a Confederate spy in the American Civil War. She operated from her father's hotel in Front Royal, Virginia, and provided valuable information to Confederate general Stonewall Jackson in 1862.

Courtesy of Bing Images, microsoft.com

www.ingramcontent.com/pod-product-compliance
Lightning Source LLC
Chambersburg PA
CBHW071252170626
46809CB00001B/185

* 9 7 8 0 6 9 2 0 4 5 1 2 1 *